I0555755

Amy's Amazing Adventures
(Across Time and Space)

Author's Note

This is a work of fiction. Names, characters, businesses, places, events and incidents are either the products of the author's imagination or used in a fictitious manner. Any resemblance to actual persons, living or dead, or actual events is purely coincidental.

Vivaeris, LLC
www.vivaeris.com
Amy's Amazing Adventures (Across Time and Space)
©2014 Juliet Chase
All rights reserved. This book or any portion thereof may not be reproduced or used in any manner whatsoever without the express written permission of the publisher except for the use of brief quotations in a book review.

Juliet Chase
Amy's Amazing Adventures (Across Time and Space)
ISBN 978-1-939361-04-2

Front cover design by www.ebooklaunch.com

Contents

Prologue

Deep in the bowels of the universe, the forces of darkness began stirring. Throughout the thirty-nine planets, sixteen parallel universes, five alternate realities, and the space-time continuum in general, strange things began to happen: crops blighted, children took sick, and telemarketers began appearing everywhere in unusual numbers.

Due to the very nature of the space-time continuum, this was not observable as an historical event. However, generations had simultaneous nightmares of the reverberating screams of a man caught in mortal combat in a small, steaming South Asian jungle. He would emerge physically unscathed, but with hard eyes and a hatred against all those that had sacrificed him to the night… and the rabbits.

1

The Adventure Gets Started

Amethyst Belinda Clarisse Daffodil Evangeline Fredericka Gregson (called Amy by her friends and even some enemies for what should be obvious reasons) tripped gaily down the wide white marble front stairs of her home, Riparian Hall, only to be met at the foot by the frowning face of her fat, nasty uncle and guardian, Greg Gregson (who, coincidentally, was also sometimes called Amy by certain people under circumstances it's best not to get into). Uncle Greg was a short, corpulent man dressed in what he clearly considered to be the height of fashion: pale pink pantaloons with a green waistcoat and yellow jacket embroidered all over with purple cabbage roses. He was too out of fashion by everyone else's standards to even be termed a fop, and so his appearance was usually described with a wordless wince. His lank brown hair was carefully oiled and brushed to conceal a rapidly spreading bald patch that unfortunately had not yet spread to his eyebrows. A perpetual pouting frown marred a face that was otherwise unremarkable.

The general unspoken consensus among those that had met Greg Gregson was that it was best not to look directly at him if one wanted to preserve one's eyesight. Amy rather thought that the lowered heads and averted gazes had given him the mistaken impression that he was a powerful and feared member of the local gentry. His demeanor had subsequently taken on a new level of pomposity, previously only found among members of the royal family. He stood now, frowning up at his pretty and vivacious niece, who owned everything he considered rightfully his, as he had told her several times with asperity over the last few weeks.

Completely oblivious to the fact that in a few days she would be fleeing for her life across the desert sands of an alternate plane of existence, Amy's long, graceful fingers nervously played with the delicate gold pendant at her neck. In an attempt to subdue her rebellious nature and avoid a painfully dull lecture on the subject, she cast her luminous violet eyes toward the black and white inlaid marble floor of the foyer and sighed. It was going to be one of those days. She was not going to be able to escape to the stables any time soon. Thick locks of gleaming auburn hair fell forward to brush her cheek and hide her expression from view.

"Missy!" roared Uncle Greg. "You are to get down here at once!"

"Yes, uncle."

Keeping her eyes demurely on the floor, she gathered the skirts of her white, sprigged organdy gown in her left hand and slowly descended the remainder of the steps, but running abreast of her fat uncle at the last step as she could go no further. From there she glanced down into his bloated, florid face and repressed a shudder. A pungent aroma of cheap, musky cologne wafted up, along with the subtler notes of body odor it was probably meant to conceal. Uncle Greg didn't hold with too much washing. How could such a creature be related to her charming, beautiful parents? His meaty hand clamped down on her upper arm and she found herself being dragged past several disapproving ancestors in the Long Hall and toward the front drawing room. She was a tall girl, standing some six inches above her uncle, but he outweighed her by at least ten stone.

"You will be accommodating to Squire Hambottom, who has come to make you an offer and take you off my hands, or else!"

"But uncle, I don't want to get married just yet, and certainly not to someone I don't even know!"

"Nonsense! You'll listen to your elders and do what you're told!" Uncle Greg's voice rose to a shrill tone as he opened the drawing room door, thrust her into the room, and closed the door again.

Amy rubbed her arms absently in an attempt to warm them. The front drawing room was dim and chilly, being on the northwestern corner of the house. It smelled faintly of mildew and disuse. Her uncle was too cheap to allow fires to be laid after the first of April, although Amy was suspicious of what was actually billed to the estate in her name. In theory she was the owner of the house and all its contents, but by law was not allowed to manage her own possessions. So the room remained largely unused and was decidedly stale. She frowned at the unfairness of it all.

In its heyday, the front parlor had been a cool summer retreat dressed in shades of Nile green silk and cream linen. The furnishings were in the Egyptian style, with crocodiles and sphinx heads on every possible surface. Now the room smelled of mildew, and the aptly named Squire Hambottom sat in the only sturdy chair in the room, a large crocodile-festooned gilt monstrosity near the fireplace, and was clearly out of his element. He did not rise at her entrance, as a gentleman should, but continued to worry his handkerchief between his soft, pudgy fingers. A near match for Uncle Greg in age and physical appearance, dressed all in a dull brown, he did not look like a man in love, more like one under a great deal of pressure without sufficient mental resources to get himself out of the fix. The squire passed for local gentry due to a lack of other applicants and a need for someone to attend the local assemblies, but those were really his only qualifications. He was essentially a pig farmer, and not a particularly good one. He was, in Amy's opinion, a dead bore. She had not been aware until her uncle dragged her in here that the squire was even aware of her existence, or that he and her uncle had anything more than a nodding acquaintance over the card table at the local monthly assembly.

After hearing the click of the lock in the door behind her, Amy gritted her teeth and seated herself in a delicate side chair on the far side of the room. She then endured a painful and awkward half-hour interview with the aptly named squire, during which she said nothing at all. Her eyes wandered around the room. Dust motes danced in the air where the sunlight managed to penetrate the smudged windows and heavy curtains. The drawing room was faded and in desperate need of redecorating; it was really quite embarrassing. She kept her mind occupied with what colors she would prefer if she should ever gain control of her own house and fortune, while the squire continued to mumble. Perhaps a French blue with cream stripes? Maybe something warmer, like peach with a pale green…

A brief pause in the squire's mumbled monologue enabled her to excuse herself on the pretext that she was needed in the kitchen. She escaped the room via the servants' stairs tucked behind one of the silk panels, which Uncle Greg probably didn't even know existed. So as not to have actually lied, Amy did stop in the kitchen, which also happened to be the one route back to her room where she would be sure not to encounter Uncle Greg. As she dashed through the cavernous room below stairs, she rolled her eyes at Mrs. Fitchley, the cook, who handed her a jam tart with a kindly smile as she went past. Amy knew that the servants, too, hoped for better days ahead.

Her mind racing faster than her feet, Amy hurried to her bedchamber on the third floor by way of yet another set of servants' stairs leading from the kitchen and threw herself facedown on the high bed groaning into the pillows. What was she to do? She knew she wasn't a biddable girl, but neither had she ever been faced with anything truly requiring open rebellion. She had not expected such a development and was in no mood to be married off to some fat, smelly pudge of a man. Someday she would find the mate that could keep up with her high spirits and sense of humor, one who would see her as an Incomparable and move mountains if it made her happy. It would be nice if he were incredibly handsome and had a slew of entertaining relations to make up for the deficit of hers as well. She rolled over on her back to continue this fantasy, but try as she might, she couldn't quite put a face to this paragon of manhood.

But enough of that—now she must take the reins and deal with avoiding Squire Hambottom, preferably for the rest of her life. She sat up and swung her feet over the side of the bed like a little girl. At best she had only prolonged the situation without having agreed to marry. Or had she? She was pretty sure that not saying anything could not be construed as an official agreement, but things could get nasty and her uncle wasn't known for understanding the fine points of logic. Amy mentally reviewed what had just taken place.

"Miss Amy... er... house... Land... Pigs... Ummmm. Errrr... see... you... Pigs. Errr."

In between furrowing his brow like he was preparing to plant turnips up there and staring at his handkerchief, the squire had cast a few lascivious glances at her slippered feet while licking his overly endowed lips. It did not make her feel any warmer to him. Amy didn't know what hold the squire had over her uncle, or if Uncle Greg had some other scheme afoot that required her to be gone from her ancestral home. She wouldn't put it past him to do something so horrific that she would be unable to undo it. She would have to come up with a drastic plan to save herself and quickly. Being ruined and forced to live on a pig farm was not something she was prepared to surrender to without a fight.

Mulling it all over, she didn't think she had time to call on any of her now happily married school friends for assistance. They would be eager to help, she knew, but it could take weeks for a letter to track them down on their endless schedules of European trips and house parties. Happy people are so much harder to get in touch with.

Flinging herself off the bed with unladylike haste, she struggled to think of a solution. The more she thought, the angrier she got. Her violet eyes flashed as she paced her room so that any fly on the wall might well have taken refuge in fear of being incinerated by the resulting sparks.

Lacking precognition of afternoon talk-show self-analysis, she was not aware that she was manifesting her internal motivation and was subconsciously thrilled with the thought of adventure and getting out of the house that never saw any visitors. So instead she worried her full upper lip with her pearl-like teeth and thought murderous thoughts at her evil uncle while wearing a rut in the carpet.

Was it really too much to ask that she be allowed to live in her own home and under her own direction? Life was so unfair.

Amy did at least know that she was restless. There was very little to do in the house, as there was no money with which to arrange a dinner party, redecorate, or go shopping. She had read everything in the library within the first week home, and the neighbors stayed away, not knowing her well enough and knowing Uncle Greg entirely too well. She was, quite frankly, bored. She wanted to go on a Grand Tour and discover things—perhaps bring back treasures to the British Museum and give a talk at the Royal Society. Something along those lines, anyway.

Amy's recent return home had been somewhat sudden although long anticipated in the abstract. It had only become reality when a new and radical rule had been established at Miss Marchant's Academy for Young Ladies of Quality in Bath. Suddenly realizing that ninety percent of her pupils were over the age of nineteen, she consulted her registration books and discovered that all of the young ladies in question were orphans with inattentive guardians paying the bills. Fearing a sudden loss of income if new and younger students could not be admitted due to the lack of available bedchambers, she consulted the local justice of the peace, whom she had secretly been sweet on for over twenty years (that's really all that need be said about Miss Marchant). A subsequent court order required that said guardians present themselves within the month and retrieve their charges. The court made no provisions for what should happen to these young women beyond that, correctly assuming that any evil doings would take place in another jurisdiction.

There was a general upheaval of emotions when the young ladies learned of this new development. For two weeks there was a flurry of packing, exchanging addresses, and a great deal of speculation. As they were whisked away in carriages and curricles, they all promised to keep in touch, and Amy thought she had come out somewhere in the middle so far. A few had been sold by their guardians to houses of ill repute then rescued by dashing, wealthy gentlemen and married happily. But still, was that worth the risk? How many dashing gentlemen did London contain? Others had to soften and cajole young, handsome, arrogant (and unrelated) guardians who then fell at their dainty feet prostrate with love. Thank God Uncle Greg was out of the running for that. And she didn't think she wanted the average dashing gentleman anyway. Without knowing quite what she was looking for in a husband, Amy sensed that she would someday meet someone different, someone who could show her new worlds and adventure, someone who could appreciate her passion for reading naughty stories in the original Greek. Clearly he wasn't going to make an appearance at Riparian Hall anytime soon. Perhaps she would have to set out to find him herself, but she rather thought she'd like to get in some adventures on her own first.

Amy was well aware that she was not a typical young woman, most of whom seemed to live for nothing more than a fine and frequently updated wardrobe and achieving the marital catch of the Season. She had often wondered whether her hoydenish nature was inherited like her violet eyes from her mother or had been formed at the loss of her parents when she was only five. They had been traveling home from London to be with her at Christmas when the carriage had inexplicably been thrown from the road. Their bodies had never been recovered, believed to have been drawn down into the freezing lake. Only pieces of the carriage and two terrified horses remained on the bank. Within days, her nasty uncle, who had never been welcome at Riparian Hall when her parents had been alive, had arrived and moved in forthwith. With now only vague memories of happier times, Amy had been separated from her nurse and sent off to school within a week. Holidays after that were usually spent at the school or on improving educational field trips. She hadn't minded. While she missed her nurse and the orchard at home during the summer, she knew that there was nobody waiting there who cared for her. At the school she had felt remarkably comfortable with her group of orphaned school chums, most of whom also had rebellious and spirited natures. But in truth they had been together so long and repeated some of the same pranks so many times that things had become a bit stale.

At times like this, she felt the absence of her parents more than ever. Their images were faded slightly in her memory as though they were born of her imagination rather than reality. She had spent very little time with them, as her mother preferred the gaiety of the city but wanted her child to grow in the clean country air. She remembered her mother's eyes like violets in the snow when she kissed Amy good night. She could recall her regal bearing and slight accent that she had not heard on anyone else's lips. Where had her mother come from? Her uncle always referred to her as "that dreadful heathen tart," but that wasn't particularly helpful. She would have to remember to look in the library later to see if there was anything noted in the family history.

Having now created a definite track in the jewel-toned Persian carpet in front of the bed, Amy stopped pacing. There was no help for it: she must escape the house, and the sooner the better. With that very basic plan in mind, she lay back down on the bed with her arms thrown wide to refine the details.

Later that night in the gloomy recesses of her bedchamber, she dashed off a note to her former nurse, who was now living in a cozy cottage in the north. There were no other options— she would have to become a governess, and Betsy could be relied upon for connections and a temporary place to stay. The note was understandably riddled with exclamation points and underlining. Amy was nothing if not emphatic in everything she did. She tiptoed softly out into the dark corridor and placed the letter on the silver salver in the hallway for a servant to pick up in the morning. She cursed softly when her knee bumped the hall table, but nothing stirred in response. She frequently corresponded with Betsy, so her uncle would not be suspicious of this outgoing missive when he franked it with her house seal. Amy was a bit nervous about the whole governess idea. She knew she wasn't likely to find a good position without previous experience. She really hadn't spent any time around young children, but how bad could they be? Her needlework and painting were abominable, and she was too pretty to be accepted into households that contained temptable men— she'd heard all about that from some of her school chums. And what man wasn't temptable? Letters from her adventuring schoolmates had given Amy a broader view of the world than her teachers ever had, but given that this knowledge was all gained from other young ladies, it was perhaps a bit skewed. Consequently, she had become somewhat cynical and overconfident of her knowledge, as restless young ladies are wont to do when surrounded by uncles of inferior intelligence.

She would just have to find a way to make it work. With her resolve firm, she changed into her lawn nightgown embroidered all over with tiny blue forget-me-nots, blew out the candle, and crawled under the covers, her mind churning over the endless possibilities for adventure that lay ahead.

The next day, when Sally, the upstairs maid, came in to open her curtains, Amy pleaded a headache and requested a breakfast tray in her room. Pulling herself up against the many down pillows while she waited for Sally's return, Amy wondered what the day ahead would bring. She felt ready to take on the world and prove to everyone that she was capable of managing her own affairs.

When Sally came back with the fully laden breakfast tray, Amy was wound so tight with anticipation it was all she could do to remain placidly beneath the covers. She wanted to get started right now. She managed to thank Sally with a languid voice in hopes of not alerting the staff to her excitement.

Well fortified with ham from the home farm, eggs, and toast, Amy contemplated her upcoming departure. Once the maid returned for the second time and cleared the dishes, Amy got dressed and began implementing her plan. Being careful not to be seen by any of the upstairs maids, she ventured out of her room, down the hall, and up the creaking stairs concealed behind a baize door that led to the attic. At the top, another heavy oak door was closed and locked. Having found the key recently in the housekeeper's room after she departed the premises in a huff, Amy had come prepared, quickly unlocking the door with the heavy iron key she slipped inside. Closing the door softly behind her, Amy heaved a huge sigh of relief, as she knew that no one would come looking for her among the cobwebs. She would have to step lightly, though. The servants would probably think it was ghosts and not investigate, but there was always somebody that couldn't resist a mystery. The attics spanned the entire topmost story of the house. Round windows dotted the long walls, which were really more to do with the exterior appearance of the mansion than lighting the dim and cavernous storage area. Thick cobwebs hung from the rafters and there was a heavy coating of dust on everything, including the floor. Clearly the servants felt safe in shaving this space off their cleaning rounds. She glanced around, wondering where to start. She had not been up here that she could remember, having little interest in old broken bits of furniture and castoff toys. The main attic chamber was huge and dark, with hulking furniture covered in Holland cloths. Illuminated only by the light from the grimy windows set far apart, she felt alone in a desolate world and a little excited at the same time. She did her best to restrain the onslaught of sneezing that erupted as decades of dust were stirred up, but a few tiny achoos slipped out anyway.

When the urge to sneeze finally abated—to be replaced by a slightly runny nose—Amy brought her focus back to the task at hand. She headed deeper into the central room with some trepidation, picking her way around the obstacles and periodically brushing cobwebs out of her face. By the time she reached the small back room, she was filthy and shaking from suppressing so many screams of distaste. Some ancestor had clearly been overly fond of hunting; his former kills were arranged on one wall, with their glassy eyes following her. Why didn't someone just throw them away? She certainly wasn't going to be taking them down to hang in the drawing room.

After rearranging some precariously piled boxes so that they would not topple over on her, she began to search. The first trunk she opened contained dainty baby clothes, the next ball gowns from the previous century. She paused a little over these; they really were lovely and might come in handy for a masquerade, but no, governesses did not attend masquerades. She pouted slightly with self-pity as she folded the brocade gown back where it had come from. Resolutely, but with a little sigh of regret, she closed that trunk and moved on. The fifth box held what she was looking for: simple garments suitable for a youth of middling income. She sorted through the pile and then, fearing that her plan would be unmasked if she had too much evidence in her room, glanced surreptitiously around before whisking her dress and petticoats over her head. She knew she was alone up here, but wasn't used to disrobing in such unfamiliar surrounds and with those animal eyes… She quickly tried on several possible outfits, stifling more sneezes from the rising dust before deciding on the brown stuff trousers and jacket. She found a wool cap in the very bottom of the trunk, and with this bounty in her arms carefully made her way back to the main attic door. She gingerly retraced her steps back to her room, where she bundled the clothing into her secret hiding place beneath the loose floorboard by the fireplace and proceeded to wait impatiently for evening.

2

Amy Makes Her Escape

Amy kept herself occupied while waiting for darkness to fall. She reread her favorite gothic novel, The Sinister Secret of the Saracen Sisters. Midway through, just as one of the sisters found herself in the depths of an abandoned oubliette, Amy took a break to get something to eat. She took the servants' stairs back down to the kitchen so as to avoid running into Uncle Greg and begged some roast beef, cheese, and fresh bread off of Cook. She piled her bounty high on a delicate pink china plate, grabbed a small jug of cider, and scurried back to her room. Nibbling on a piece of beef, she went back to her book, quickly becoming entranced in the drama even though she knew perfectly well how it ended. After turning the last page, she closed the book with a satisfied snap and got up from the window seat where she'd been curled up.

The shadows were lengthening, so she went back to pacing her room and planning the exact path of her escape. She hoped she was making the right decision to leave. If nothing else, there didn't seem to be any reason for her to stay. No suitors would come near with Uncle Greg around, her friends were all far away, and there was very little to do that could be done with absolutely no money. Eventually, after what seemed like eons, the shadows stretched into twilight. She gathered her feather pillows beneath the bedclothes and shaped them into some semblance of a human form. Standing back near the doorway, she glanced toward the bed and nodded with satisfaction. If she were the upstairs maid she would take the form for the deeply slumbering version of herself, which gives a good indication of how poorly Amy was equipped to be a member of staff.

She quickly dressed herself in her boy's costume and took a moment to admire it in the long mirror in the corner. Somehow she didn't quite look like a boy, but hopefully in dim light and at a distance it would do. She took a few practice swaggers across the room. This wasn't so bad. Maybe she would give up skirts altogether and become a revolutionary of some sort. Did they still have pirates anywhere? Could girls become pirates now? She rummaged in the trinket box on the dressing table and pulled out the one thing she didn't want to leave behind. Amy hung her mother's delicate pendant around her neck. It was the one piece of jewelry she truly cared about, and the one thing she had of her mother's that was really personal. A warm feeling of well-being always came over her whenever she touched it. Feeling somehow that her mother's spirit was guiding her, she moved quickly to complete her preparations.

Amy carefully retrieved the few coins she'd managed to save over the last year and put them in her reticule, which she stowed beneath her shirt. She gathered her long auburn hair into a twist and fitted it beneath the wool cap. It seemed somewhat lumpy, but she wasn't quite desperate enough to cut off her hair. At last, she stuffed a pretty green day dress, her hairbrush, and a book of poetry into a small bag, cast one last look around the room that had sheltered her since infancy (metaphorically speaking, considering most of her life was spent at school), and thought "good riddance" to herself. She blew out the candles and opened the chamber door. Knowing that her uncle was always away from home on undisclosed business Thursday evenings and that the ill-managed staff always took advantage of this, she walked directly down the main stairs, making no attempt to muffle her steps. She made her exit from the house by the grand front door, since this was the farthest exit from the kitchens where the servants were already getting themselves drunk on the cooking sherry.

Her feet crunching softly on the gravel in the drive, the half moon shining over her shoulder, she walked carefully around the house to the side yard. In the dimness of the stables, she finally located Tom, the old coachman, who by sheer coincidence was the only servant who could not stand cooking sherry and was a little antisocial anyway. It took some time to convince Tom that she was the lady of the house and not some stable boy intent on a prank, but finally she won him over when she took off the cap. With a few graceful tears and half her precious hoard of coins, Amy managed to persuade him to drive her to a coaching house on the outskirts of London. From there, she would be able to get a message to Betsy without revealing her destination to anyone making inquiries later.

She waited impatiently inside the stable doors while Tom hitched up the horses and brought the old coach into the yard. Taking pity on his arthritis, she waved him to stay on the coach seat, wrestled the heavy door open, and climbed into the moldy interior. She couldn't remember the last time this coach had been used, but it must have been before her parents' death over fifteen years ago. She barely had time to get the door shut again and they were off. As they rambled down the avenue lined with stately elms, now ghostly shapes in the darkness, the adrenalin began to wane and she drifted off into an uneasy sleep.

As one might expect, Amy awoke suddenly when her elbow banged sharply against the side panel. The coach was shaking violently from side to side. With no idea how long she'd been asleep or where they might be, she slid off the bench to the floor between the seats. The coach was hurtling headlong into the night. Amy crawled back upon the faded velvet seat and hung on to the coach strap for dear life as she tried to see out the dingy window into the darkness. She wondered if old Tom was even still onboard or if other forces were guiding her to certain doom. Gusts of cold wind penetrated the close confines of the old coach and sent an eerie shiver down her spine.

With great difficulty, Amy managed to regain her footing and stand up on the seat. She banged on the trapdoor overhead without completely losing her balance.

"Tom? Tom, what's happening?" she called. But there was only ominous silence as the coach continued to sway violently. Amy could see nothing but blackness out the windows. There was nothing taller to stand on and she was not tall enough to see out the trapdoor without assistance. She sank back down on the bench seat. Was she to die then like her parents, without accomplishing even one adventure? Fate was too busy at that moment to reassure her, but within five minutes the coach slowed to a sudden stop. Her heart rate slowing to a level slightly below extreme panic, Amy stared out the window but still saw only blackness. She was just about to disengage the door handle when the door suddenly burst outward.

A masculine hand in an elegant, slim-fitting, black leather glove reached into the interior of the coach. It gestured peremptorily.

"Miss? Would you care to step outside for a moment?"

The highwayman (for what else could he be?) had a roguish tone to his voice that was warm and appealing, but Amy wasn't a complete idiot. On the other hand, she didn't see how she could do much by remaining in the now stationary vehicle. Gingerly taking the extended hand, she exited the coach. Reaching to gather her skirts as she stepped down, she suddenly remembered that she was dressed in boy's garb. But he had jut called her "miss." How had this man known she was female? What was going on?

Alighting softly on the ground, she searched frantically for a familiar landmark that would give her some idea of where she was. The highwayman was the only clear shape within view. Dressed completely in black with a black cloth covering the upper half of his face to the rim of his hat, he stood with his arms crossed and a bemused expression on the lower half of his face. He had a slim but wiry build, standing just a few inches taller than she. After a careful perusal of her from top to bottom, his lips quirked slightly before he released her hand and spoke.

"Well, Miss Gregson, I can recommend a good dressmaker if you like. I think you'll find this season's fashions more flattering."

"How do you know who I am? And how did you know I'm a lady?"

He rubbed his firm jaw with his gloved hand and said thoughtfully, "The answer to both of your questions is the same, and I'm afraid I can't tell you that right now. But just in case you ever feel like running away again, you should know that there's no way any man would mistake you for being of his gender." He grinned as a sliver of moonlight illuminated his face, reflecting off amused blue eyes.

Amy darted her eyes to the side and thought to take her chances and flee into the night, but just then two burly individuals approached from either side, effectively blocking her against the wall of the coach. One of them held a lantern, and she could see that they were in a flat area by the side of the road but tucked away from view by a copse of trees.

"Aye, Sor Midnight, the coachie's tied up and the hut's ready for the little liddy," said the one on the right.

"Tom!" exclaimed Amy, feeling guilty that in the confusion she had completely forgotten about him. "Sir Midnight!" Couldn't he have thought of something more original? It lent an almost comical note to the unfolding events. How could she relay this to her friends and have them take it seriously? For some reason she wasn't feeling overly concerned for her safety, which may not have been particularly wise.

"Relax." Sir Midnight spoke condescendingly, not knowing the focus of her concerns. "There's no call for hysterics. Your coachman has merely been removed from the temptation of attempting to assist you. He'll be returned unharmed to your stables, and no, in case you're wondering, that's not my real name, but Tiny and Little Tim here have some difficulty with my real one so we keep it simple."

Amy wasn't sure if she wanted clarification on that cryptic remark or not. "Look, I don't have any money or jewelry. Please, can't you let us continue on our way? I'm expected at my destination shortly."

"Expected at three in the morning? Where exactly were you headed?" he said with some skepticism.

She shook her head mutely, not putting it past Uncle Greg to question highwaymen in his attempt to keep control of her fortune.

"Well, never mind, for you won't be getting there tonight. And it's not your money, jewels, or virtue that I'm after." He grinned ominously, but it lost much of its intended effect when the lantern light caught the reflection off of the pendant around her neck. Sir Midnight's eyes bulged out slightly and his mouth fell open. Amy wondered if he'd been taken by a fit, but after a moment he reached out with an index finger to trace the design.

"Why, what an interesting piece. I'll take that pendant, if you please."

Amy wasn't about to give it up easily. As far as she knew it was just a bit of frippery with no more value than the sentimental kind. "You just said you wouldn't take my jewels!"

"I lied. Highwaymen do it all the time."

He didn't even sound sorry about it. Surely he was just trying to be cruel and wouldn't take such a small thing. When she made no move to unfasten the delicate necklace, Sir Midnight stepped forward lightly and gently snapped the gold chain in two. As he slipped the pendant into an interior pocket of his shirt, she caught only a glimpse of it disappearing before she reached up to feel her bare throat. She felt curiously naked without it.

"While I would love to stay and further our acquaintance, I'm afraid that someone is waiting for news of your whereabouts."

"Who?"

Not answering, he reached into another pocket and brought out a black silk cloth that he began to wrap around her eyes. Bringing her hands up, she grasped his wrists, pulling them down. "Well, if that's the way you want it, we can do that part first, I guess." Stepping back, he broke her grip, and reached

out a hand to the man on his left, who handed him a few feet
of rope. With a move so fast that Amy didn't see it until too
late, he fastened her two wrists together with the rope and tied
it securely. The blindfold went on as he'd intended, and she was
no longer able to make out even dim shapes. "I'm afraid we will
have to leave you nearby for a while, my dear, just until I can
ascertain where to deliver you." He picked her up and flung her
over his shoulder. The ungraceful pose was uncomfortable, but
did have the benefit of rearranging the blindfold slightly so that
she was able to see a portion of the ground they were traversing.
There wasn't much to see, really. But after a few minutes fast
walking, the hard, pebbled surface shifted to a soft, lush grass
and Amy fancied she could feel some strange vibration that was
not emanating from the highwayman.

3

Amy Makes a Discovery

Sir Midnight halted abruptly. Caught unawares by the sudden change in rhythm, Amy's nose bounced hard off of his back, bringing tears to her eyes.

"Tiny, will you get the door, please?"

Hinges creaked and Amy found herself being lowered to an upright position and then seated in a chair.

"I'm sorry for the rough accommodations, but we should be back for you in a few hours. We'll be locking you in, but feel free to try to get out of those ropes in the meantime. That should give you something to think about, anyway."

With that, she heard three sets of feet leave the small building. The door shut and a padlock rasped into place. Amy thought frantically. It must be getting close to dawn, which was coming earlier and earlier as summer approached. So she had very little time. Her uncle would be on her trail as soon as her escape was discovered. Through the narrow gap in the blindfold she was able to peer down one side of her nose, and could just make out the ropes on her wrists in the gradually lightening gloom. Bringing her hands up to her mouth, she began anxiously tugging at the ropes with her teeth, hoping to reverse the complicated knot pattern the highwayman had woven.

After about ten minutes' perseverance, shivering slightly in the pre-dawn cold and with several slips resulting in biting her tongue, Amy felt the ropes give way. Reaching up, she slid the blindfold over the top of her head, where it made a sort of hair band for her now loose and disheveled locks. She stretched out her arms and legs. All that bouncing in the coach had caused her to stiffen up considerably.

Glancing around, she found that she was in what appeared to be a small shepherd's hut. There was no furniture beside the chair but a small, broken pallet frame in the corner suggested that it had been some time since it was occupied. A single tiny window on the opposite wall was letting in the first rays of dawn. Amy quickly moved to the door and found that not only was it locked but that the door had been reinforced and was probably the strongest part of the entire structure. Thinking furiously, she paced the perimeter of the room. Her pendant was probably lost to her forever, but there was no reason she needed to give up her person or her adventure without a fight. Moving away from the room's perimeter, she began to pace in a diagonal, the only direction there was enough room to get a good, furious stride. After several repetitions of this, she noticed that the rough floorboards sounded differently in one corner, almost hollow somehow. With her head down, she began to walk slowly but firmly, listening carefully to the sounds of her footsteps.

When she again heard the hollow thunk, Amy sank to her knees and frantically felt around the edges of the floorboards. Finding no obvious pulls, she began inserting her fingernails between the boars in a systematic fashion. "Damn it!" She carefully extricated a splinter and stuck the offended digit in her mouth before resuming her task. Five minutes and approximately ten feet of floorboard later, her explorations yielded something rather puzzling. A lever of some sort lay underneath the shortest of the floorboards directly in front of the fireplace. There was still only a crack between it and the next, but when she moved her fingernail from left to right it definitely encountered something that moved and then slid back into place when released. But nothing else happened. Nothing popped up or out. Amy sat back on her heels to think, blowing her hair out of her eyes and wiping a dusty hand across her forehead.

Something was niggling at her memory. For some reason she was thinking about a visit in long-ago childhood to a huge mansion in the country, right before her parents died. It had been the residence of some relative or other of her mother's, she thought. She remembered an old man taking her through rooms of treasures with so many good possibilities for building forts or hiding from nannies. But she hadn't been allowed to stop and explore.

That was it. The old man had shown her a secret hiding place in a desk. Not the usual sort of cubbyhole that kept ignorant thieves out, but one that required multiple actions to be opened, beginning with pressing down a lever that could be felt but not seen. Then the desk front had to be pressed at the same time to make the very base of the desk pop out to reveal a shallow drawer.

If this were a similar mechanism, what could possibly be serving as the second release? Amy looked all around, trying to see likely spots within reach of the lever below the floorboard. There was nothing within reach of her right hand, but if she just stretched out her right foot… Glad that she was still in the boy's clothes, Amy completed the complicated maneuver, albeit ungracefully, pressing the ball of her foot firmly against the side of the fireplace.

With no warning, an entire section of flooring to the left of the fireplace sprang up on a complicated set of expanded hinges. The "door" was so carefully hidden that the irregularity of the ends of the floorboards was continued, which was why it had gone unnoticed by several hundred shepherds over the years.

Amy retracted her foot and hand into a more dignified position then inched carefully over to the gaping hole in the floor. It was a very dark hole. There appeared to be a sort of metal rung ladder against the side that looked sturdy enough, but she was hesitant to try anything without seeing where she was going. What if it was an evil sort of oubliette, like in the gruesome novels she had read at school? There could be bodies, or worse, down there. She leaned her head over and peered down. A long way down and slightly to the right, as if there was a path with a turn in it, a faint blue glow emanated from the gloom. What was that?

Amy sat back quickly—a little too quickly judging by the stars flying in front of her eyes—and contemplated her options. She could wait passively for the highwaymen to reappear, but that meant either something dire, or being returned to fat Uncle Greg, where she would probably be handed over to Squire Hambottom still tied up. She could continue to search for a more standard escape route, but casting a searching gaze around the small hut, she didn't see anything likely. The window was miniscule, the fireplace was too small to crawl up the chimney, and the door was too stout to break down. She looked back down into the hole. It was starting to appear a little more attractive.

Deciding to risk it, and figuring that in the worst scenario the highwayman would be able to see where she'd gone and come after her, she awkwardly turned around and felt around with her foot for the rung. Inching her way down the ladder into the increasing gloom, she wondered what this tunnel could possibly be for. She didn't think there was much smuggling this far inland, and even in bad novels oubliettes did not glow.

When she had climbed about twenty feet down, her reaching foot encountered nothing but empty space. Bracing herself against the ladder, she risked a look down over her shoulder. The blue glow was now so much stronger that she could see that she was at the end of a tunnel that curved around to the right. She looked back up to where she had come from, but the top of the ladder had now disappeared into darkness. The last rung where she currently stood was about three feet up from the tunnel floor. Amy hung on to the ladder for a moment, knowing that once she let go she probably wouldn't be able to get back up again. When her arms started getting tired, she made her decision. Awkwardly, she jumped down, twisting her ankle slightly in the process. Hoping that it would wear off, she rubbed her ankle briskly before gingerly proceeding down the tunnel. The floor was swept clean; no cobwebs or dust to be seen. The entire tunnel seemed to be made of smoothly packed earth. It was hard to see any details in the gloom, but she thought that there was an interlacing ribbon pattern painted on the walls. The strange blue glow got stronger and bluer with each step she took into the tunnel. With one last turn to the right, the tunnel abruptly ended at a door.

It was an attractive six-paneled door with one of the new fanlights above. On a recent school trip to London she had admired similar ones in the new mansions being built around Hyde Park. The blue glow was emanating from the fanlight and seeping through the crack between the door and its frame. She tried turning the brass knob, but it wouldn't budge. There was no knocker anywhere to be seen. Amy was now so into her adventure that it didn't even occur to her to backtrack or seriously consider why such a stylish doorway was buried so far beneath the earth. Instead, she began examining the walls around it.

Just to the left of the door, on the sidewall of the tunnel, was a small brass plaque with several little black buttons. There was writing adjacent to each button in a crabbed, odd script. The top one said simply "Araby." She pressed the button.

Suddenly, the blue glow grew darker and began to swirl with green. The swirling motion of the light moved faster and faster, casting odd reflections and shadows on the tunnel walls. Amy could barely see through the flashing light, but she reached out and tried the knob again. This time it turned easily in her hand. The door was open before she could catch her breath and think things through. With a small pop, she was sucked through the doorway and flung like a sack of wheat onto a sand dune.

4

The Prince of Thieves Has a Bad Day

After closing the door on his captive, St. Abyn St. Abyn—for such was the real name of the Prince of Thieves—also known as Sir Midnight, sauntered leisurely away from the shepherd's hut and paused to lean against one of the giant standing stones with a sigh. It was getting harder and harder to work the night shift. He hoped he wasn't getting old ahead of his time. The small building was located just on the periphery of one of England's ancient stone circles. Still holding some of yesterday's heat from the sun, the stone warmed his back through the thin silk of his black shirt. It felt good to be back in rural England, where most things moved at a slower pace. Almost like a vacation.

The sky was quickly lightening, feathers of pink and gold spreading across the open horizon. Mist lay heavy in the shallow valleys beyond the central plain, catching the early morning light. St. Abyn reached into a hidden pocket in his shirt and retrieved the pendant he had stashed there an hour previously. He laid it across his palm with the delicate broken chain hanging over his fingers. He knew this design well. What he didn't know, and greatly wondered at, was how it had ended up in early 19th-century England. He stared at it for a long time, willing the small piece of jewelry to give up its secrets. It remained mute, thin lines of gold filigree interlaced to form the Oryctolan character for "chosen one."

It was generally considered dangerous for anyone to write or wear a character of such power. That is, in the galaxy located approximately ten thousand light years and... and, well, at some other time. St. Abyn suddenly realized he didn't have the faintest idea of the Oryctolans' origins. In his day, they had been long gone, made real beyond myth and legend only by the occasional archeological find of a tablet or leafy cornice stone. The few surviving painted images clearly showed that they were not human, but how realistic those images were was a matter of continual scholarly debate. Their language had survived much longer in the popular culture because of its fashionable associations with fortune telling and soothsaying. The written hieroglyphs were known only to those few who had traveled the continuum and they didn't wear them as jewelry.

He glanced up from the pendant with a troubled look. Now what was he to do with the girl? He had only gotten involved with this adventure because he didn't trust Tiny and Little Tim to handle it without roughing the poor thing up, even unintentionally. At the time it had appeared to be a perfectly ordinary abduction for hire, now he wasn't so sure. Normally he didn't get involved in the actual front end of the business. His role was really to oversee various thieving enterprises on the five worlds and three alternate universes that made up his region. The travel and the paperwork kept him fully occupied. He was firmly established in the hell of middle management and eager to move on to bigger and better things.

His boys had been hired by the girl's uncle to watch the house and stop her at the first sign of escape. She was supposed to be handed over to some local bureaucrat for official compromising.

Unfortunate, but if he stopped to worry about the welfare of everyone touched by his business he would never get any work done. Somebody had to balance out the effects of fair business practices, after all.

Once he saw the girl and the pendant around her neck, St. Abyn had made a quick change of plan. He felt oddly protective of her, and certainly intrigued by the mystery. She was neither biddable ninny nor lightskirt, and as such deserved a little more of his attention. So he had stashed her in the transport hut while he thought about what to do. He still didn't have a clue.

The stone against his back suddenly hummed with energy and warmed to an uncomfortable temperature. St. Abyn straightened abruptly, moving away from the monolith he had been leaning against. He reached out a tentative hand to feel the stone, sure that he had just imagined the heat. It was still hot to the touch and vibrating slightly, then both sensations dissipated abruptly. "Oh, shit!" he said under his breath, and looked toward the small hut, which stood about two hundred feet outside the circle. As far as he knew, he was the only one that used this spot as an entrance portal, everyone else preferring the larger one near Salisbury. It had much better secondary transportation available, not to mention inns within easy reach. The standing stones acted as radiators to disperse the massive energy generated well below the surface. The generators only came on when the portal was activated; he had never known them to malfunction. The girl couldn't have found the trapdoor to the tunnel, could she?

Swearing violently under his breath in several languages, he ran swiftly back to the hut, fumbling in his clothing for the padlock key. Where was the bloody key? Finding it at last, innocently lying where he had left it in his trouser pocket, he unlocked the padlock and lifted the hasp to peer cautiously inside. The damning evidence of the flooring section suspended on its hinges in midair stared back at him. The girl was nowhere to be seen.

"Right, then, one Regency heroine lost somewhere in this or some other universe. Now what?"

Damning himself for his own stupidity, St. Abyn entered the small hut, closing the door behind him. He did not want to compound the situation by having his two henchmen learn more than they should. They were local employees and hadn't a clue that their boss had grown up on another planet. They were famous for not comprehending anything beyond the obvious, but he didn't want to push his luck at this point. It was clearly not going to be a good day.

St. Abyn lowered himself proficiently into the gaping hole and clambered down the metal ladder. He carefully checked out the tunnel, hoping that he had just imagined the onset of the radiators. Deep in his gut, though, he'd been pretty sure that he wouldn't find the girl—and sure enough, there wasn't a trace of her. Unlike the larger portal in town, this one did not have the latest memory technology in the control panel, so there was no way of knowing which way she had gone. Maybe this would finally get him the upgrade that he'd been requesting for the last two years. On the other hand, if he could recover her before his manager found out she was missing, so much the better.

St. Abyn retraced his steps, closing the trapdoor behind him, and went back out into the warmth of the sunshine. He was a good Prince of Thieves, looked good in black, and knew how to run his organization efficiently. He moved with confidence and purpose. Tracking adventuring virgins through the universe wasn't on his résumé. He didn't think he wanted to add it, either. Some skills are better left un-acquired, as once you have them people will keep asking you to use them. But he knew someone that needed a challenge.

St. Abyn had met Ten on an exploratory mission into the Northern Wastelands of Alternate Universe B. The naming of alternate universes was a matter of great debate, each one feeling quite strongly that they were at the center of things and ought to be A. To St. Abyn's way of thinking, his own universe was A and the rest named in the succession of his first visit. Ten was an ex-Navy SEAL that had "retired" from his own world to lick his inner wounds and generally avoid people. St. Abyn wasn't sure what Ten did with his time exactly, beyond skulking through the scant underbrush and eating beans off a knife in front of a campfire. It wasn't like there wasn't a fairly decent-sized outpost nearby with an inn. When asked why he didn't eat his meals there, Ten's only response was that he hated stew. He didn't respond when asked why he was in the Wastelands, just went back to his can of beans with a fierce look on his face. After that, St. Abyn didn't dare ask him any personal details, like what his real name was. He'd learned the hard way not to ever talk about rabbits. He preferred his facial features in their current arrangement.

Ten had the tracking skills and knowledge of the portal system necessary to find the girl. He didn't seem to do much with his days, but then appearances are often deceiving. The question was: what would it take to convince him to accept the job?

St. Abyn thought about heading back to town to get some money, then decided that time was of the essence. He didn't think Ten was motivated by money anyway, and currency was frequently a problem in alternant planes of existence. Once he negotiated with Ten he could always return to arrange the payment. He got up swiftly from the flat table stone on the ground where he'd been sitting and strode over to Little Tim and Tiny, who were sprawled on the grass snoring. Why was it so hard to get good help these days? No one had any initiative anymore. Well, except for that blasted girl, who could have done with a great deal less of that commodity.

St. Abyn poked the two giant human lumps with the toe of his riding boot. Grunting, they came awake and stood sheepishly. Deciding he didn't have time to indulge in a lecture on proper workplace decorum, St. Abyn sent them back to the warehouse office along with his horse. They acted puzzled by this, shuffling their feet and glancing about, but he simply put on his haughtiest air and stared down his nose at them. This was quite a feat, since they were both about a foot taller than he, but not being too bright, they bought it.

Once the two men, trailing the third horse, were beyond the next ridge, St. Abyn went back into the hut. He performed the gymnastics necessary to reopen the secret door, grimacing slightly at the moves required. He really was getting too old for this stuff. As he lowered himself down the ladder, he carefully closed the trapdoor over his head with one hand. He then moved quickly down the corridor to the control panel. Luckily this portal went directly to the Northern Wastelands and he wouldn't have to waste time arranging for a transfer at another station.

The third button on the panel said simply "Wastelands," but someone had scrawled above it "Damned boring." Obviously the scribe didn't appreciate the Zen qualities of endless boulders, stunted trees, and barren landscape, all in shades of dun brown. Neither did St. Abyn. The Wastelands lacked the cultural amenities and sophisticated women that he found most appealing. Violette would not be pleased when he failed to show up for their assignation that evening in London. Oh well; he'd been getting a little bored with her anyway.

With a sigh, he pushed the button and opened the door. On the other side was an abandoned section of the cellar beneath the one inn in the Wasteland outpost. Nobody had ever bothered to give the town a name, as that might imply affection and a desire to stay. The smell of stew and ale penetrated into the murky depths from the common room above. He stepped through the portal and closed the door behind him. With some luck, maybe he could find Ten, hire his services, and get back to town in one evening.

St. Abyn executed the complex steps to open the secret panel on the other side (the exact steps have been kept secret for your protection), emerging behind the stacked barrels of ale in the main basement. At the top of the stairs, and luckily before he opened the cellar door, he suddenly remembered how he was dressed. He quickly swept off his mask and hat before going through to the common room.

5

Rendezvous in the Wastelands

The Sign of the Gagging Goose was a bustling establishment. Serving wenches—dressed as all good serving wenches are, no matter what universe—were distributing bowls of stew and refilling the pewter ale tankards. The wide plank floorboards had soaked up so much spilled ale (and other substances) over the years that they had taken on a strange, smooth patina that frequently caused the unwary to get a whole new perspective. This had the added benefit of adding more ale to the floor finish and getting a big laugh from the other patrons. For some reason, this joke never palled, at least not for those safely ensconced on the benches. The owner of this fine establishment figured he saved a lot of money by not having to pay bards for entertainment, so he refused to sand the floor. Already familiar with the danger, St. Abyn minced carefully over to a small table in the shadows and breathed a sigh of relief when he sat down safely.

A buxom, red-haired serving wench was at his side, instantly plunking down a pewter bowl of stew and a full tankard. These were the only items on the menu, so efficiency was gained by not having to print up menus or returning to take orders. St. Abyn dug into the stew for a few minutes; it had been a long time since breakfast, but once his immediate hunger was past he remembered how tired he was of stew. The Gagging Goose didn't bother to try to fancy it up any, either. Picking up the tankard of ale, St. Abyn leaned back in his chair and surveyed the other patrons. Most of them were rough-looking caravan sorts, theoretically collecting the chamois skins for sale in the more civilized parts of the world. They would load up the caravans in the fall, making it down the narrow mountain pass just in time to avoid the first blizzard if they were lucky. A few of the bar patrons had the aura of "trying to blend in" that suggested they were here on other business, but none had the catlike moves that were Ten's trademark.

St. Abyn snagged the nearest barmaid with an arm around her waist as she swayed past. Beer foam drifted down onto his dark hair as he whispered in her ear, asking if she had seen the modern barbarian lately. She shook her head, two trays of beer and stew, and her flaxen braids no. This was going to take some digging, then. He hoped that Ten hadn't decided to leave the Wastelands after all this time. Shrugging, he sighed heavily and went back to his stew.

The talk around him drifted from individual conversations to group speculation about the upcoming summer festival, where all the same customers of the inn went outside to drink ale and eat stew. Something about al fresco dining made it a festive occasion, even when nothing else changed. When the patrons started to place bets for the stew-eating contest, St. Abyn got up slowly from his chair and silently made his way to the door. As it swung shut behind him, he waited a second for his eyes to adjust to the darkness before moving. It was a second too long to avoid the steel arm that now wrapped around his neck, hauling him onto his tiptoes.

"I heard you were looking for me," the low, disembodied voice whispered in his ear. He knew that voice—it was attached to the man he was searching for. This was not quite so bad after all. You could survive with a crushed trachea, couldn't you?

Unable to get a peep out, St. Abyn attempted to move his head in an approximation of a nod. Another arm came down and sort of picked him up around the waist. He found himself under the dim light of what passed for a streetlamp, being scrutinized by two glowing eyes that stayed just outside the circle of illumination. St. Abyn hated being at the disadvantage. This was how good thieves became dead thieves.

"Oh, it's you again, the nosy little guy. What do you want now?" Ten did not sound happy to see him. On the bright side, he wasn't sounding quite as violent as he had been immediately outside the public house, either.

"I've come to make you an offer."

"What kind of offer?" Ten wasn't sounding too receptive.

"I need you to find a missing girl. She… um, accidentally went through a portal."

"How on earth did that happen? The portals don't allow the uninitiated, you know that. What are you really after?"

"I told you. I need you to find this girl."

"Not interested. If I wanted to go around the universe chasing women, I certainly wouldn't be hanging out in the Northern Wastelands. Sorry you had to waste a trip."

"She isn't just any woman. She was wearing a royal pendant."

That caught Ten's attention. Everything about him seemed to focus and home in on St. Abyn. He set him down on his feet but kept a hold on the neck of his jacket.

"You're sure about the necklace?"

"Yes, I'm sure. It's the same symbol." Suddenly remembering

he still had it with him, St. Abyn took it out of his pocket and handed it over. "Here, take a look for yourself."

Muttering something about people who talked too much, Ten took the pendant and gently laid it on his left palm. He glanced at it briefly in the dim light of the streetlamp then tucked it into the breast pocket of his fatigues. "We'd better go back to my place where I can look at this better." Turning quickly and silently on his heel, he faded into the night. St. Abyn hurried after him. He hated hurrying after anybody; so not an alpha male thing to be doing. He had hopes of breaking out of middle management in the near future, but if he couldn't take charge of situations like this his superiors weren't likely to hand over the promotion. On the other hand, Ten wasn't likely to be part of his 360 reviews, so he could probably spin it to his advantage when he had some time to think it through.

Ten was living in the smallest hovel on the outskirts of town, or at least that was how it appeared on the outside when they arrived. It wasn't much better on the inside, but it was clean and had several modern appliances and gadgets not known anywhere else on the planet. Ten flicked on the light just inside the door. Seeing his quarry clearly for the first time in years, St. Abyn was once again reminded that he didn't compare favorably in the height, weight, or fierceness categories. Ten's wheat-blond hair and all-weather tan invariably drew attention away from the more svelte thief, which was just fine for lifting valuables but less so for asserting managerial authority.

Like most alpha males, Ten was oblivious to any such comparisons. He had a small study set up in the back of the house with a comfortable chair big enough to suit his long frame, a big desk, and stack of rolled-up blueprints in the corner. It was to this room that he led St. Abyn.

"Hey, what happened to that tent you were living in? I thought you didn't want to go soft?"

"Do I look soft?" Ten's voice held humor and menace at the same time.

St. Abyn had learned enough from his prior experiences to know better than to answer that in the affirmative, even if it were true—which it wasn't, of course.

Leaving St. Abyn standing by the desk, Ten moved blueprints around to find the chair underneath then sat down, turning on a desk lamp as he did so. He reached into the desk drawer with his right hand and pulled out a jeweler's loupe. He silently flipped the pendant over and began examining the backside. St. Abyn certainly couldn't see any difference between the two, the workmanship was so fine. Ten leaned in closer to the pendant, furrowing his brow. "It would appear…"

"Yes, what?" St. Abyn leaned forward.

"You're blocking the light."

Chastened, St. Abyn moved back and Ten continued.

"The jewelry is mere frippery beyond the symbolism of the design. The power lies in this nanochip on the back. My guess is this is a key of some sort, to a door or to information. Possibly both."

"What does that mean?"

"I don't know," Ten answered slowly, "but I think it's time we went and found your girlfriend."

"What is this going to cost me?" St Abyn inquired with trepidation. He would have to pay any price, but perhaps Ten didn't know that yet.

"You buy the supplies, don't steal from me, and don't think that I'm going to leave before my questions are answered."

"Deal." With a deep sigh of relief, St. Abyn couldn't believe that he'd gotten off so lightly. Although he didn't much appreciate the remark about stealing, it wasn't like he'd actually succeeded in picking the man's pocket five years ago.

St. Abyn took the list of supplies Ten handed him and showed himself out of the house before heading off to the supply depot/ general store to see what he could acquire illegally tonight before returning in the morning to pay for what he couldn't. No sense in paying more extortion money to the bloodsucking corporations than absolutely necessary.

6

The Navy SEAL Heads Out

No one, including St. Abyn, knew that Ten had spent six months living with the hunting cats of Felis IV, the largest sentient predators of any known universe. It was there that he had honed his already formidable skills and taken on the feline nuances of movement that made him such a lethal enemy.

Those six months of tracking targets in the jungle had brought back memories he'd rather not have to think about. But he'd made some new ones too—"playing" with the young kits had honed his reflexes to a new high and earned him a reputation for scratching ears in just the right spot. Someday he would complete the mission that had taken him there for training. He expected to die in the process, so he wasn't in a huge rush.

After making sure St. Abyn was clear of his established security perimeter, Ten retreated into his living quarters and began assembling his pack. On the return trip from the small bathroom with his shaving kit, he found Wallace, the grumpy, banged-up old tomcat, sitting squarely in the middle of the bag. The cat had wandered in from the barrens one night a few years back, his dark apricot fur covered in scratches, with a few new holes in his ears and a look in his green eyes that dared anyone to pity him. He'd let Ten administer some first aid, though, and eaten the small bowl of stew he'd offered. He'd come around a bit after that, like an old friend that shows up to chew the fat, so Ten had named him after a former drill sergeant who hadn't been much for conversation either.

Although he'd never admit it, even to himself, Wallace was the real reason Ten had upgraded from the tent farther out in the Wastelands to the broken down old shack on the edge of town. That particular winter had been so exceptionally cold that the cat had actually snuggled up to him in his bedroll. Hating to see Wallace give up his dignity like that, new accommodations had been arranged.

Without conscious thought, Ten's blunt finger now found the exact spot behind Wallace's ear that caused his eyes to close and a silent rumble to occur deep within. Ten frowned a little at the reminder that Wallace now depended on him for more than he'd used to. Getting up in years, he slept under the big desk chair more and hunted less—coming by for a small bowl of stew on an almost daily basis.

"Buddy, I can't take you with me."

Wallace's eyes opened with an accusing glare.

"You'd have to ride in the pack, and I don't know how long this is going to take."

Wallace got up and resettled himself, facing the other direction.

"Look, I get it. But you'll have to stay with Sally while I'm gone. She'll treat you right—probably even find you some cheese." One notched ear twitched at this. The sad fact was Wallace loved cheese, but it gave him really terrible gas. Ten drew the line at having to smell that stench in his semi-civilian life. Sally, on the other hand, was a bit more open-minded. She was one of the barmaids at the Gagging Goose with a long history of pursuing aloof males. She'd struck out with Ten, but made more progress with Wallace once she'd discovered his weakness. Wallace allowed her to pamper him occasionally, and they'd formed an odd kind of friendship.

Ten continued gathering items to take with him on the bed and straightening up what remained. As he rolled up the blueprints of the Lost City he'd tracked down a few years ago on Labrerke IX, he wondered if this was the prelude to his final mission—the one requiring his ultimate sacrifice. Unconsciously his hands clenched over the roll of paper at the memory of the pain that felt like every cell in his body was being reorganized. His jaw clenched, he forced his hands to relax and smooth out the paper breathing deeply as he did so. He'd take one day at a time, just like he'd learned to all those years ago when his life had changed so drastically.

He'd always been a bit of a loner, but even Ten recognized he'd taken things to the extreme when he'd relocated to the Wastelands. He hadn't known anything about portals and alternate worlds before that fateful night in the jungle. Until then he'd naively thought that terrorists and serial killers were as bad as it got. His family was long gone before he even joined the service, and he could hardly tell his old friends about his new depth of knowledge. They'd have just looked at him with pity and unloaded all his guns. The Wastelands generally let people be, unless of course you went chamois hunting out of season—that could get you a one-way ticket to the penal colony on the smallest moon of Serelius VI.

He efficiently finished up his packing and gathered Wallace into a padded carry bag he'd fashioned from discarded chamois skins he'd found along the main trade route through town. Exiting the shack, he didn't bother locking the door. He wasn't sure he'd be back, and there wasn't anything of value in there anyway. He and Wallace headed off to the pub, where Sally welcomed the cat with open arms. Snuggling into her generous bosom, Wallace cast a meaningful glance back toward Ten, who, despite his acknowledged sins against the feline community, was already heading through the back door leading to the cellar and the portal without a backwards glance.

7

Amy Meets the Sheik of Araby

While her would-be rescuers got themselves organized, Amy processed her immediate situation. Sitting up, she twisted her torso to look all around. Seeing only rolling golden sand dunes in all directions with endless blue sky above, she closed her eyes and shook her head to clear her vision. When she opened them again, the sand dunes were still there. Whatever door she had come through had disappeared under the fine golden grains. Getting carefully to her feet, Amy looked around for some kind of landmark and then stood helplessly for exactly two minutes. It was warm and getting warmer with each passing breath. The sky was a clear deep blue with not even a trace of wispy clouds. The sun shone brightly just above the horizon line, making the golden sand glow. She should try and find shelter as soon as possible. Miss Marchant had spent considerable time lecturing the girls on the social evils of freckles. She started walking, keeping the sun to her back to minimize the damage.

Amy walked for hours. The dunes rose up to meet her and then fell away. The sun went from warm to hot to sweltering, burning her eyes as it reflected off the sand. Each dune looked just like the one before it, and no clouds disturbed the even blue of the sky. The sweat gathered between her shoulder blades and bosom and dripped down.

Well, it seemed like hours, but in reality was only about forty-five minutes. She paused for a minute on the rise of a dune, wishing she had some water and wondering how long it took to die of thirst. She was beginning to feel a little sorry for herself and wishing that there were someone out there to mourn her death. She could picture it now—her pale, lifeless body draped gracefully across the slope of a dune, the blowing wind teasing at her curls while gradually covering her corpse with sand. A tear pricked the corner of her eye.

Without any warning, a ululating gang of men on white horses came thundering over the next dune. Before Amy could even blink or think to move out of the way, she was caught up by a powerful arm and slung behind the first rider. Bouncing as the horse galloped and clutching somewhere around what she guessed to be the man's midsection rather than slide off the horse, she pondered this latest development. She was still too hot to make much of a protest and wasn't all that sure this was worth complaining about until she had more information. Glancing over her shoulder, she could see that all of the men, roughly six or seven, were swathed in white. The long robes parted over white trousers bound up by the lacings of fine white leather boots. What was with all the white? Then again, compared with Uncle Greg's recent forays into more colorful fashions, perhaps they had the right idea after all.

The group continued riding over the dunes, the horses stretching their legs in a relaxed gallop. Although their hooves made little noise on the shifting sand, the chattering and singing of the men drowned out her brief attempts to find out where they were taking her. Just as suddenly as the riders had appeared, the horse she was on abruptly halted as though hitting an invisible wall. It began walking calmly, continuing in the same direction as before. Amy finally got her chance.

"Um, excuse me, where are you taking me? What's happening? Why did you stop?"

The man she was so intimately clutching replied without turning his head, which made his words difficult to catch as they drifted out across the sand.

"We are taking you to Lord Kalil, of course! He had notice of your arrival, but since we moved the camp recently he thought you might get lost."

His voice was pleasant enough and his English perfect. Where was she?

"As for why we are stopping… She wants to know why we are stopping!" He raised his voice so the rest of his group could hear him.

All of the men grumbled and she thought she caught the words "Damn females!"

With exasperation thick in his voice, he continued, "We are slowing down to a crawl because my wife, Fatima, has put her foot down and complained to Lord Kalil about the dust in camp. She says there is only so much that can be shaken out, and that if people don't gallop through, everything will stay clean. She bribed him with his favorite pastries, so now we must walk the horses within two sand dunes of camp." He grumbled and sounded most put out, but Amy was beginning to perk up. There was at least one woman at their destination, and a lord that could be bribed with pastries somehow didn't seem as evil as one that couldn't.

The slower speed allowed Amy to look around her—there was still nothing to note about the sand dunes. But the horses! They were magnificent. All white, like their riders, and easily sixteen hands high. The saddles were of tooled red leather, with multicolored tassels decorating the pads and halters. The nearest one pranced a little when he caught her admiring eye.

Reaching the crest of the second sand dune since the sudden deceleration, Amy peered past the man's shoulder with eager curiosity. Gazing down into a slight sand valley that was filled with glittering tents in jewel colors, her eyes widened with awe at the sight. Multicolored silk pennants flew from the central tent poles, fluttering in the breeze. The other riders separated from the group, still walking the horses while grumbling loudly in the direction of a slight woman wearing fine silk robes of gold and red, stirring something over a campfire in the middle of the campground. She didn't appear to notice them, but her lips quirked slightly in amusement.

Amy was taken up to the largest tent of all, a gleaming silver palace with scarlet ribbons fastening the fabric panels to the poles. This surely was what the new Brighton Pavilion was hoping to imitate—a veritable Xanadu with Kubla Khan about to emerge from one of the tents. Her captor/rescuer dismounted then reached up to Amy, but she ignored him. Her eyes grew wide as she took in all the tents and people hurrying by. She reached out to touch the silver damask that made up the tent wall. It gleamed and shimmered with a woven design of peonies and chrysanthemums. She had never seen such beautiful fabric. What her friends would give to have just one gown out of something so magnificent.

A man stepped out of the silver tent. He was slightly built. Like his compatriots, he was dressed all in white, but without the enveloping robes. A fine linen shirt was tucked neatly into his trousers and the neck was open to reveal his deeply bronzed throat. The bright sunlight glinted off of deep blue eyes that seemed to command her gaze. He had a certain presence about him that distinguished him from everyone else in the camp. A warm but puzzled smile shaped his firm lips.

Correctly assuming that this must be Lord Kalil, Amy didn't wait for introductions. She was past any pretense at formality after a very trying day.

"Where am I?" she demanded.

Lord Kalil's expression grew more puzzled. "You don't know? This wasn't your intended destination?" he inquired politely.

"I pushed a button marked Araby and then suddenly was here. Where is here?" Amy's voice was growing a little shrill. Although generally a delightful girl, she did have a slight tendency to get whiny when she got overtired.

"Ah," was Lord Kalil's only response.

He paused for a moment, fingering his well-shaped chin.

"Why don't you come in, get cleaned up, and have some food. We can figure this out after you've had some rest." He held the tent flap back invitingly.

"But where am I?"

He raised both eyebrows. "Why, Araby, of course. Didn't you just say that was the transport you called?"

A little stunned, Amy finally accepted the lift down from the horse and preceded him into the tent. Her eyes grew wide at the even broader rainbow of colors and the glitter of silver and gold ornaments that decorated the interior. The floor was covered with overlapping Persian carpets in a rainbow of hues. There were silken pillows scattered everywhere and sumptuous draperies everywhere else. Gold and silver vases and bowls were piled on every flat surface. She stopped just inside the entrance. Not sure what the protocol was for paying calls in tents, she pondered the possibilities. Where did one leave a calling card with no foyer and no butler? Then again, she was still dressed in her boy's clothing and her reticule had been left behind in the coach. And, for that matter, she hadn't exactly come of her own free will.

Meanwhile, Lord Kalil had turned his back and was rifling through drawers in a low bureau, muttering something about Fatima and her incessant cleaning. "Ah, this might do!" He held up a sort of shift with sleeves in a brilliant shade of pink with gold trimmings. He held it out for Amy to take.

"I will keep my own clothes, thank you all the same!"

"Well, I'm not going to tie you down and strip you." He looked a little terrified at the thought. "But it would definitely be in your best interests not to be mistaken for a boy in this camp."

"Why?" she asked warily.

"They make the boys handle the camels. Nobody wants to do it, so the young boys get the short end of the stick. Nasty beasts."

Not sure if he was referring to the boys or the camels, she decided it didn't really matter; he had made a convincing argument. Gathering the clothing into her arms, she looked around for somewhere she could go to change.

She saw a crimson damask cloth heavily embroidered with gold and pearls suspended near one wall. Ducking behind it, she found she was in a bathroom of sorts. A large porcelain tub was set up in the corner and various thick white towels were piled on colorful cushions. Amy quickly stripped and, dipping a small towel into the bathwater, gave herself a fast sponge bath, keeping a wary eye on the end of the suspended cloth serving as a door. Had she been more conversant with tents, damask, and the theoretical concepts of backlighting, she would have known that her actions were completely visible through the cloth to anyone in the tent that cared to view them.

Luckily for her, there wasn't anyone else in the tent. Lord Kalil had said something about ordering dinner before stepping out, and she hoped there wasn't going to be anything too foreign and strange to deal with.

Clean and dressed in the pink silk garment that seemed like a skimpy corset cover to her, Amy began exploring the tented palace. Her outfit didn't leave much to the imagination, due to it having previously belonged to a young woman who frequently volunteered to be abducted for a night or two. Amy poked through the same drawers that Lord Kalil had been rifling and finally found a square cloth that she draped around her like a shawl, covering her shoulders and décolletage. She didn't care if he thought her rude for going through his belongings. She was not going to go about like some opera dancer. Swathed in the additional white silk draperies edged with silver gilt, she continued her explorations, trying not to think about what might be coming next on her adventure.

The tent was like something out of Lord Byron's poetry. Silver and crimson damask sheltered any inhabitants from the scorching rays of the desert sun. A soft scent of sandalwood perfumed the air, emanating from various boxes inlaid with jewels and silver. Silken cushions of green and purple with dangling tassels were artistically arranged around the perimeter, while a six-foot chandelier festooned with cut-glass brilliants hung suspended from the peaked center of the ceiling. Amy thought she had seen one very like in the new assembly rooms in town. Her slippered feet sank into the dense pile of the Persian carpets as she moved slowly into the room. The only light was the fading sunlight filtered through the crimson damask of the interior wall, which gave everything a muted, rosy glow. In a far corner she spotted tall bookcases filled with leather-bound volumes. She eagerly scanned the spines, looking for something familiar that would make her feel more at home. One wall began to billow inward as an evening breeze off the desert gathered force. She took down a slim volume of poetry that she hadn't read and settled herself in a pile of cushions.

The light soon made it too dim to read. There was still no one else in the tent. When she peered out of the small opening between the tied tent flaps, she saw that darkness had fallen. There was the pale glow of what she guessed to be campfires at some distance. Even though she was ravenously hungry, she did not feel like exploring the rest of the camp. Surely someone would remember her and bring some food?

Her eyes now drooping with weariness, she spied a long purple cushion that looked long enough to fit a settee. It was tucked out of the way in the far corner with mounds of smaller cushions all around. Plopping herself down, she arranged the small cushions to her satisfaction and quickly fell asleep.

Amy woke groggily to the sound of male laughter and the dim glow of lamplight. Someone had draped a light silk coverlet over her, and she was glad, for the wind had dropped the warm overtones of the day for a slight chill. Still only half awake, she listened to the conversation.

"Shhh, keep your voices down. I don't want to wake her up."

"But sir, what are you going to do with her? She doesn't belong here!"

"No, but accidents do happen. Why, there are rumors that my great-great-grandmother came to us the very same way. She used to talk of a great city by the sea. You won't find one of those in Araby."

"But my lord!"

"Relax; we will give it a few days to see if anyone comes to retrieve her before we move camp as scheduled. If no one does, then maybe I'll marry her."

The last was said with some humor, but Amy wasn't amused. Marry her! How dare he! She did not want to spend the rest of her life in a tent (or on a pig farm). Lord Kalil continued, unhampered by the mental outrage aimed in his direction.

"You know, that might not be such a bad idea. She intrigues me. She reminds me a little of Fatima, all that fiery passion. I wonder if she can make pastries?"

Amy closed her eyes again and groaned silently. This was only getting worse. She must not panic. She would wait and see what tomorrow brought. Maybe she could find a way to get back home, or convince someone to help her. Her stomach gurgling, she rolled over on the cushion to feign sleep. But her movements had caught the attention of the group.

"Miss? Miss? You might as well stop pretending and come get something to eat. Fatima has made honey and nut pastries in your honor. She said you are too skinny."

Amy sat up with mixed emotions while rubbing her eyes unconvincingly. Skinny! Of all the nerve. But the concept of sweet pastries was too good to ignore, so she rose and gathered her makeshift draperies around her.

Eight or nine men were gathered in a loose circle in the middle of the tent with a colored glass lantern and several platters of food. They were all seated cross-legged, still dressed in their white garb from earlier in the day.

Lord Kalil shifted slightly to make room for her at his right, gesturing with a graceful hand, and said, "You know, I don't even know your name. What shall we call you?"

Amy was aghast at the lack of manners—that anyone would demand her name in such a way without a proper introduction! But then she remembered. There wasn't anyone here to perform that task and likely would never be. Who knew if she would ever see her home again? Sighing sadly, she knelt and said simply, "You may call me Amy."

"Ah, Aimee! So lovely. Let us quickly do introductions. These are my men. This here is Abdul that you met earlier, he is married to Fatima, then Tariq, who minds the horses, Omar, Rashid, Abir…"

As Lord Kalil continued to name the men, Amy's attention was suddenly caught and held by the platters of food in front of her. Here were juicy sliced tomatoes, fragrant concoctions that smelled deliciously exotic, and the pastries! Oh my. They were shaped like little tents, with the golden, flaky crust falling away to reveal the honeyed interior. She looked around for a plate. Abdul, seeing where her attention had fallen, gently nudged a silver charger in her direction.

Not used to dining without servants, Amy hesitated slightly, looking around before reaching out to pick up the tomato slices with her fingers. Shocked at her own daring, she was even more astounded that nobody else seemed to care. Amy started to think that maybe other worlds weren't so bad after all…

She reached out again and grabbed two pastries, biting into one as there was a sudden scramble for the pastry platter among the group.

Warm honey and almonds filled her mouth and delighted her taste buds. Amy closed her eyes in ecstasy and therefore missed seeing that all other eyes in the tent had just become riveted on her mouth and fingers. The sudden quiet had her quickly popping her eyes back open, wondering if she had just committed a fatal faux pas. Edging her tongue around her lips, she caught a drop of honey in the corner of her mouth and licked it away.

Fatima bustled in a few minutes later to begin clearing away the dishes, and Amy could see that she was beautiful as well as talented with pastries. Dark, almond-shaped eyes surveyed the dirty dishes with a tsking look that softened when they came to Amy. Gesturing slightly, Fatima helped Amy to rise and led her out of the tent and showed her the location of a very small tent that housed the necessary and a small washstand. After taking care of business, Amy found her way back to the silver tent, only to find that all the food had been cleared away and a small bedstead had been set up to one side. A pale yellow drape was held invitingly back with a pink ribbon. Other similar drapes separated a much grander bedstead, which Amy correctly interpreted must be Lord Kalil's. Shocked again by the amazing impropriety of it all but too tired to make a fuss, she undid the pink ribbon, letting the drapery fall into place, and crawled into bed. A few minutes later, someone came through and blew out the candles in the central chandelier. As the tent fell into darkness, Amy slipped into a dreamless sleep.

The next day, Amy made quick progress through the bookcases she had spotted earlier. Most everything was in foreign languages she didn't know, so she was left with a treatise on crop rotation, a couple of novels she had already read, and a cookbook devoted to what else? Pastries. Everyone in camp was very busy—even Lord Kalil was off training horses—so Amy felt a little miffed being left to her own devices. She perked up slightly when Fatima came and fetched her for dinner in her own tent—it seemed that last night's gathering was a special occasion and not the norm. Fatima's tent was royal blue with silver trimmings and in a bit of disarray. Fatima apparently did not speak English, but the disparity of why she didn't but Lord Kalil and his friends did was not explained. Amy was happy enough to have female company and so didn't concern herself with the limited conversational avenues. Amy gathered from Fatima's hand gestures that the camp was moving soon and there was much work to be done to get everything stored properly beforehand. She wondered how she was ever going to get back to the portal if they were relocating, but she wasn't sure what to do about it.

Her anxiety got the better of her later that night when the tent and compound were dark. Snuffling a little into her pillow as the tears leaked out the corners of her eyes, Amy felt sorry for herself and her fate. She didn't like not knowing things or how things operated, like the portals. She was used to (and quite frankly enjoyed) being more intelligent and better informed than those around her.

Lord Kalil's soft voice appeared at her elbow. "Aimee, whatever is the matter?"

"Nnnothing," she snuffled.

"It does not sound like nothing—perhaps a pastry would help? I believe there is one left over in the tin…"

"No, thank you. It's just I… I don't want to be here."

Lord Kalil sat back on his heels. "Well, where do you want to be, then?" He sounded just the teensiest miffed.

"I don't know!" Amy wailed, and the tears began in earnest.

Lord Kalil started feeling around in the dark for the pastry tin.

"It's just that I don't really want to go home. There's nobody there for me. My friends are all busy with their own lives and new families. My uncle is hideous and nobody will let me do what I want! Just like here."

He tried again: "What do you want to do that nobody will let you? I made sure you have the freedom of the camp, and admittedly it's light on nightlife, but I quite enjoy it."

"I want to adventure and travel and see foreign lands!"

"Um, isn't that what you are doing?" he ventured cautiously.

"Well, yes, but that was last week. Now I'm ready for a new place."

"I can help there! We are moving camp at the end of the week—it will be all fresh sand dunes you have never seen before!"

Amy groaned with frustration. "It's not the same. I want to get on with my life. Not live your idea of my life. There is more to see and do than eat pastries!"

Lord Kalil gave up and went back to bed with a sigh.

8

Amy Escapes (Again)

A week later, as she was returning from an urgent trip to the smallest of all the tents, Amy found her feet automatically carrying her toward the big silver tent she was starting to think of as hers. She was half asleep and it was still dark, so it took her a few seconds to realize that a horse had just ridden into the camp at something resembling a gallop. No one else was around to take the horse, so he was left in the center of the rough alley between tents with his reins dangling. His rider strode rapidly toward her own destination, the master tent. As he disappeared under the flap and candlelight flared, Amy suddenly realized that this was her chance. Moving as quietly as possible, she ran to the horse and gathered the reins in her left hand. Somehow managing to hurl herself into the padded fabric saddle, she settled herself atop the tallest horse she had ever ridden. The robe she was using as a night rail rode up over her knees. The horse danced about but did nothing else to challenge this unorthodox and unfamiliar rider.

Although she had been treated like everyone's sister since arriving in the small tent city, Amy was eager to reclaim her independence. There had been several hints over the last few days that she might like to try her hand at making pastries, and Lord Kalil had begun kissing her hand while gazing into her eyes at every opportunity. As charming as she found Lord Kalil, she didn't want to marry him (not that he had asked yet, which had also piqued her temper a little). It was time to rescue herself and get on with her life. Sitting around on silken cushions all day was not her idea of fun.

Amy was an excellent horsewoman, there not being any other sport considered ladylike, and in any event it suited her temperament. So she did not hesitate to turn the horse and urge him to a gallop, heading in the direction he had just come from. She spared a brief glance back as the horse cleared the edge of the compound, but all was silent; a brief flicker revealed that lamps had been lit in the big tent, but that was all. Amy turned her head back and willed more speed to the horse. She didn't know where they were going, but surely divine intervention was possible? She was certainly becoming experienced at escaping.

A few hours later, the sun peaked over the horizon, lighting the sky and the desert with a clear, golden light. Amy could see now that the horse she was riding was all white, with a long mane that had been braided with gold and scarlet threads to match the elegant tasseled halter. This was not a common messenger horse, no matter what world it was on.

As the sun rose higher in the sky, Amy began to wish that she had thought this out a little more carefully. She was wearing only the thin pink shift Lord Kalil had given her the first day, which she had taken to sleeping in since it was a little too immodest and too pink to wear anywhere else. She had no scarf to cover her head and neck from the burning rays of the sun, and most important, had no water.

They passed nothing but sand dunes for what seemed like

hours. She only knew they were not going in circles because they continued to ride toward the sun. Several times she had thought she saw a grand city in the distance only to have it flicker and dissolve as they crossed the next sand dune. Her tongue felt swollen and cottony in her dry mouth, and the horse had slowed to a near walk. It was too late to try and turn back; they would never make it. Her only hope was to continue going and hope that either they came across another settlement or were followed and taken back. Her eyes flickered as another mirage formed, but this one was different. It looked like two figures rather than a city or a lake. They didn't disappear, instead growing larger, as the horse that Amy had begun referring to as Snowball, in honor of a childhood kitten, ponderously crossed each dune.

The two figures resolved themselves into men that were standing and watching her as she approached. The taller of the two had a muscular build and sculpted features that revealed no emotion. His wheat-blond hair was darkened by sweat, but otherwise he seemed unaffected by the sun. Neither was dressed in the white robes that now seemed ubiquitous, but rather strange trousers and jackets that were completely foreign to her. The big blond man reached an efficient hand up to grasp the bridle just as Amy and Snowball drew level. Snowball immediately began to perk up and began lipping the men's baggage in search of water. Amy's glazed eyes also began to clear as the man held a clear, flexible bottle up to her lips. She took a grateful swallow of the cool water and then glanced again at the two men.

"You again!" she sputtered, almost choking as she tried to swallow and gasp at the same time. The sight of the highwayman quickly revived her energy and her ire. "What are you doing

here? How dare you tie me up and leave me in that hut? If you
hadn't interfered I'd be safe with Betsy now instead of dying
of thirst in the desert completely un-chaperoned! I'm ruined!"

Gesturing the water bottle at the other man, Amy kept going.

"And you! Who are you? And what are you doing associating
with this kidnapper? Did you know he was working with my
Uncle Greg to force me to marry a pig farmer! Well? Did you?"

The man quirked an eyebrow at the highwayman and simply
waited for Amy to run out of steam. "I go by Ten. If you are
what we think you are, a pig farmer is the least of your worries."

Affronted by his lack of respect for her predicament and the
role the highwayman had played in it, Amy glared.

After some winsome conversation on the part of the
highwayman, St. Abyn, and practicality setting in with Amy,
the three headed over an adjacent sand dune to a rough shelter
that provided some shade. There was a small well and a watering
trough for the horse. Gratefully sitting down and leaning into
one of the hewn supports, Amy wondered if she had gone from
the frying pan to the fire, but didn't have enough energy to
resist the incessant questions from the two men.

In close proximity, Amy began to realize just how very big
and solid this new man was. It rather unnerved her. Despite his
size, he moved with an innate grace and efficiency of movement
that drew the eye. He wasn't like anyone she had ever seen
in Bath or London. He must have felt her staring, because he
looked up suddenly from the pack he was excavating to stare
back at her. She dropped her eyes in confusion and hoped it
was too hot to blush.

St. Abyn started in on the questions. "What was your
mother's full name?"

"Hester Imogene Jonquil Katherine Lisle Meredith

Nisqually." Amy said it very fast as to get it all out without taking a breath. "Why?"

"Ni-squ-al-ly," St. Abyn repeated carefully and thoughtfully, putting a slightly different intonation on the syllables. He and Ten exchanged a glance.

"I thought they'd all died out?" Ten said to the other man, seeming to ignore Amy entirely.

"Me too. When the Quark invaded, the entire family was massacred in the Imperial Palace. But there were rumors…"

Ten crooked an eyebrow inquiringly.

St. Abyn continued, "There were rumors of a youngest child, a girl of about three whose body was never found. It was thought that she was simply too small to withstand the blast of a plasma gun and she simply… disintegrated."

Amy's eyes widened in horror.

"The others were pretty messed up, so that supported the theory. There have, of course, been several pretenders claiming to be the long-lost daughter, but none of them could gain access to the sacred portal. Once the colored contacts were removed, none of them had the family's violet eyes."

One pair of blue and one pair of suspicious green eyes swiveled to stare at Amy's violet ones.

"I wonder…" St. Abyn said.

"I'm wondering the same thing," Ten said grimly. "If she is, we could finally gain access to the lost world. We might find the answers we need there."

Amy had finally had enough. "What are you two talking about? And why are you staring at me like I'm a prize fish?" She sounded just a touch exasperated.

Ten and St. Abyn exchanged another look. As if by mutual decision, Ten took the lead and said carefully, "Oh, not a fish, sweetheart. But definitely a prize, and possibly the savior of the universe."

"Hunh?" Actual words had finally escaped her.

"We think you might be the only living descendent of the Imperial Royal Family. The only acknowledged link through the known universes. They had special status with the Oryctolan so that as individuals they did not exist in more than one world at a time. Forty-five years ago, there was a brief parallel alignment of the planets through all the universes. A group calling themselves Originists seized the moment to stage a coup. Armed with ruthless alien mercenaries known as the Quark, they took advantage of a rare occurrence. Because of the alignment, the royal palace was well, fully present everywhere. Normally, the family was careful to disperse members to different sectors and universes, but at that moment they were all vulnerable. The main guerilla movement was quickly defeated, but the royal family was gone. And with them, the ability to gain access to the Core. Chaos gained a foothold and has been gathering strength ever since. You and your necklace are the key to regain entry to the Core. We may still have a chance to reverse the damage before it's too late."

Amy's head was reeling and her eyes were wide. Alternate universes? Imperial Family? "But, but…"

St. Abyn finally spoke up. "Why don't we get out of this forsaken place and go someplace cool where we can explain everything?" He took a small gadget out of his belt pouch and flipped open a lid. He poked at it a bit before saying, "Ah, yes. About a quarter of a mile that way"—gesturing vaguely to his right—"we should find a portal with access to Chichen. Should be lovely and cool this time of year." His face cheered up suddenly as he added, "And they have really good ale."

"Wait a minute! Why should I go anywhere with you? And what about the horse?" Amy asked with concern.

"Well, you didn't seem to want to stay where you were at, did you?" Ten raised yet another sardonic eyebrow at her (he really only had two, but they seemed to multiply quickly). "You should be aware that your enemies will now know you exist. You're a prime target for assassination attempts."

"Enemies! I don't have any enemies. Well, not if you don't count Mathilde Carrington-Psmythe, the horrid cow."

St. Abyn chimed in. "You do have enemies—entire phalanxes of them, now determined to finish the job they started. You should have stayed put in that hut; if you hadn't gone through the portal this would all be a lot easier."

"Then you shouldn't have put me there in the first place! I wasn't out looking for portals—I was headed to London and then on to Betsy."

"Children! Enough. Let's deal with the current situation, please." Ten brought their attention back and St. Abyn and Amy both pouted a little. "The horse will be fine here. Someone should be along shortly to see who came through and they can collect her. Horses are no longer allowed through the portals."

"Why not?"

"Um, due to an unfortunate incident." St. Abyn cleared his throat and studied the horizon hard.

"Oh." Amy understood all about Unfortunate Incidents. She had caused a few of her own. Out of politeness for a fellow sufferer, she did not inquire further, but stood up and began walking. She really didn't have much of a choice. As far as she knew, the only place that was here was Lord Kalil and his camp. Perhaps another world would offer better opportunities to strike out on her own. She was tired of people telling her what to do. Somewhere there had to be a place where she could direct her own destiny. And she missed her friends.

With his highwayman's suave demeanor, partly natural and partly developed during several management-development offsites, St. Abyn tucked Amy's arm through his and began leading her over the dunes as though they were entering the finest ballroom in London. Silent and with a slight glower, Ten followed behind with the baggage.

Gradually the dunes gave way to outcroppings of rock the same color as the sand. There was still no vegetation, but a narrow path was becoming visible in the firmer surface. Small lizards skittered and disappeared as they approached. Rounding the corner of one really big rock, the little group was suddenly in a narrow ravine. As they entered the little box canyon, the walls rose to impossible heights over their heads, casting the entire space into shadow. The canyon floor widened slightly at the back in front of a pedimented doorway that was carved into the center of the far wall and surrounded by exotic floral carving. Classical columns and inlaid niches flanked the opening. The niches were filled with exquisite white marble statuary. The figures were about three feet tall and looked like ones Amy had seen at the British Museum, except that these all had the heads and ears of rabbits.

Amy stopped so suddenly that Ten nearly ran into her. Only his natural grace stopped him in time. His breath warm on her neck, he muttered, "I really hate this place." She glanced back at him inquiringly but he said nothing further. His eyes were fixed on the building ahead. Standing so close to him, she felt the restrained strength that fairly emanated from him. His gaze still on the rabbit figures, he moved around St. Abyn and Amy, heading for the open doorway. "Come on, let's get out of here!" Amy resisted the need to go examine the sculptures more closely—there was something very compelling about them, as though they were trying to tell her something.

The three of them entered the cool cavity carved into the rock face. Amy could just make out an elaborate inlaid marble floor in the dim light entering from the clerestory windows, which must be above the level of the canyon somehow.

"What is this place?"

Her voice echoed quietly with awe in the cavernous chamber as she craned her neck to see the details of the ceiling.

A long time later, she heard a response.

"Once upon a time it was an Oryctolan temple. Now it's a portal site." St. Abyn was the one to answer her question. When she glanced back at Ten, who was once again bringing up the rear, she saw that he had faint white lines bracketing his firm mouth. Amy thought she could see his pulse jumping beneath his square jaw. He gave the impression of a man under considerable tension.

There were no other windows in the small room, nor furniture, just a layer of desert dust on the floor and the carvings on the stone walls. There was another portal here? Where could it possibly be? She didn't have to wonder long, as Ten moved with purpose toward the back wall of the small room. He placed one hand on the inlaid image of a palm tree, one foot on a camel in the floor design, and gestured with his free hand.

"St. Abyn, get the other release, would you?"

St. Abyn pressed a small hexagonal piece of tile near the door, and suddenly the whole wall moved back about three feet, revealing a doorway similar to the one that Amy had accidentally found—except this one had a Moorish ogee shape at the top instead of a fanlight. It was painted yellow, but the same blue glow was seeping out around the edges.

"Timer set?" Ten asked St. Abyn curtly.

St. Abyn turned a small dial by the door and nodded. Ten stabbed at a button on the panel with a blunt index finger. The door began to glow green. Ten turned the handle and stepped through. Amy was about to get a little affronted by his rudeness at not ushering her in first, but then thought better of it. She stepped through carefully and felt St. Abyn close behind her.

As the blue glow slowly faded in the now empty temple chamber, there were three quiet beeps and the wall panel gradually slid back in place.

9

Traveling on Chichen

This time when Amy walked through the portal, she stepped lightly onto a forest floor carpeted with moss and small ferns. It smelled damp and loamy but not strange. It was almost anticlimactic. Tall lavender trees hung with more moss covered the small glen, filtering the soft sunlight in what appeared to be late afternoon. Pale green orchid-like flowers hung in long tassels from the trees, scenting the air with vanilla. A small creek burbled around the perimeter of the clearing and little birds were hopping to and fro. A gentle breeze teased the air, which was refreshingly cool after the arid stillness of Araby.

It was a tranquil spot. Amy would have been glad to linger for a while and look about for wild flowers, but the two men clearly did not have pastoral relaxation on their minds.

"How far to that inn?" Ten asked St. Abyn.

St. Abyn got out his pocket device, poked some buttons, and said, "About ten miles. I don't think we'd better risk it."

Ten nodded and set off through the trees, not looking back to see if they were following. Amy was now thoroughly confused. St. Abyn had started after Ten, but looked back over his shoulder to see Amy frozen in the same spot. "Come on, then," he said, not unkindly.

"Where exactly are we going? I thought someone was going to explain all this once were through the portal?"

"We'll explain everything once we've set up camp for the night. You don't want to be in these woods after dark without a really big fire." His voice got quieter as if he were afraid of something overhearing. "Come on, I don't want to lose Ten's tracks. He knows these woods better than anyone."

Amy's eyes grew wide as she tried to peer between the dark vegetation to see what was there. She couldn't see anything out of the ordinary, but hurried to catch up with St. Abyn anyway.

About twenty minutes later, just as she was wishing she had better footwear, they walked into another small clearing. It too was festooned with moss and ferns. Amy couldn't help but wonder why they couldn't have stayed in the first clearing. Ten already had a small fire going in the center and was gradually adding larger pieces of wood. Feeling a little chilly in her thin silk, Amy went closer to the fire, rubbing her arms. Ten raised a sardonic brow, then reached behind him and tossed a small pack to Amy. "Here, make yourself useful." Bending down, Amy looked in the pack and saw a small pot, a few utensils, and some neatly wrapped packets of foodstuffs.

"Um, what should I do with it?"

Ten eyed her speculatively. "Can't cook, huh? Thought that was only a problem with modern women."

Amy wasn't sure how she'd been insulted, but was quite confident that there was an insult in there somewhere. "Why don't you just explain why we are here? And why I can't go home now?"

"I think I'll let your boyfriend do the talking."

"Boyfriend! He's no friend of mine, he abducted me!"

"But came after you," St. Abyn reminded her with a cheeky

grin as he came up to the fire with a load of dead wood. "That's what friends do." He dropped the wood by the fire and put one hand over his heart dramatically. "I'm hurt that you should have so little regard for our time together."

Amy glared.

Once the fire settled down into a bed of hot coals, Ten efficiently put food in the pot and rested it in the glowing mass. It was a simple meal, consisting mostly of beans, but it was better than no food at all. They ate quietly, too tired to converse. Amy was so exhausted that she forgot to interrogate the other two with her list of questions. Nothing seemed so important as eating and then going to sleep.

They all cleaned up their dishes, and as Ten was adding wood to the fire, Amy began looking around the rough campsite, trying to guess where they were going to sleep. Gently bred young ladies were not generally exposed to camping under the stars, and certainly not with two previously unknown men that she wasn't related to. Ten ignored her nervous glances, although his lips twitched occasionally as he reached into another pack and took out three tightly folded blankets. He handed one to St. Abyn, who shook it out and refolded it into a rough pallet. Spreading it on the ground near the fire, he lay down and stretched. Ten did the same with the second, spreading it so close to St. Abyn that there was no ground visible between the two. Amy stood there fidgeting. Ten glanced at her then gestured to the blanket. "You're in the middle."

"Thank you, but I think I might be more comfortable on the other side of the fire."

"Sorry, darlin', it's too dangerous out there."

"What danger? I haven't seen anything!"

"And you probably won't, even when the harblob come into

camp and drag you away."

"What's a harblob?"

"Sort of a cross between a giant rat and a scorpion."

"Oh."

Amy wanted to think that he might be lying to her, but he seemed extremely confident. She sighed and sank down to the wool blanket, trying to keep her knees and ankles decently covered as she did so. Ten was busy spreading his blanket next to hers, and St. Abyn appeared to be already asleep. She lay down carefully, trying to keep all her body parts within the narrow confines of her blanket. It was warmer now than it had been before the sun went down, which seemed odd. Ten lay down with a groan and his breathing quickly steadied into a low, slow rhythm. Amy was too wrought up to sleep. She gazed up at the few stars visible between the branches and wondered if the harblob were even now gathering outside the camp. What kind of sound did they make? Did they maybe give off an odor? She sniffed the air experimentally but didn't notice anything exceptional. There was a giant boulder poking her lower back. She could feel the warmth of the two men on either side, so she dared not roll over and try for a more comfortable position.

She spoke into the darkness: "Where are you taking me?"

Ten answered quietly, "We have some critical business to take care of."

"That doesn't answer my question."

"You wouldn't understand it if I did—it's a world far away and in another dimension, but we need you to get there."

"How come?"

"Because it appears you are of royal blood. Basically, your body is a key and nobody else can get through without you."

Amy rather liked the concept of being royal and special but

was less enthused that it was coming across as though she were a commodity. "What if I don't want to come?"

"Where else would you go?"

He had her there. She was back to feeling frustrated at her lack of knowledge.

"I want to learn about the portals. I want to go exploring."

Ten groaned. "That's all the cosmos needs right now. A young innocent traipsing about without a care in the world, or the universe, attracting assassins everywhere she goes." The sarcasm was thick enough to slice.

"And what happens when you land in another world with no money? Or not speaking the language?"

"Well... I've managed well enough so far, haven't I? And everyone speaks a little French. I'm sure I can get by."

This time Ten didn't even try to control his exasperation. "Do you really think a little schoolgirl French can get you safely around the universe?"

"Yes." She paused to rein in her temper. "Miss Marchant said that every civilized society speaks French."

"And what about the uncivilized ones? Because that's mostly what we're dealing with here. Maybe when this is all over St. Abyn can hire a governess or something for you to teach you what you need to know to take your place as the last member of the Royal House. I don't know."

"Why can't you do it? Now?"

"Because I have a mission to complete—one ordered by beings far higher than the Royal House, and since that mission requires you as well, you've been drafted."

It wasn't a term familiar to Amy, but the tone came across perfectly clear. She sniffed forlornly and rolled over in the other direction, trying to get a little more comfortable. Clearly independence would have to wait a little while longer.

Amy woke with a start and found herself enveloped in comforting warmth. She lifted her head and heard a muttered "Ow!" as she connected with something hard. She was wrapped in Ten's arms. With her head tucked under his chin, she had been brazenly spread across his broad chest. She looked around from her still-prone position. And to make it worse, she had clearly rolled off her blanket and onto him. Mortified, she attempted to disentangle herself. Ten sighed heavily as he rolled her off onto her blanket before the knee that was seeking leverage on the ground did some real damage. His hands may have lingered a little longer than necessary, but nobody was at hand with a stopwatch. Amy looked away in embarrassment, only to see St. Abyn leaning on his elbow, grinning.

"Well, well, not so maidenly shy after all, hmm?"

Amy resorted to glaring as she felt a burning blush move up her cheeks, and was just about to issue a sharp retort when there was a rustle in the woods. All three froze and stared in that direction. There was another rustle. Ten moved smoothly into a tensed crouched position while St. Abyn and Amy quickly rose to their feet. A figure burst out of the underbrush and into the clearing. But rather than the grotesque animal she had been expecting, this one resolved itself into Lord Kalil.

He came to rest a few feet from the three people that were now standing amidst their tumbled blankets in the dawn light with almost matching bemused expressions on their faces. Ten had relaxed his pose but was still rubbing his stubbled jaw and wincing where Amy's hard head had connected earlier. Amy stood gaping, her eyes swinging from Lord Kalil to St. Abyn and back again. They were indistinguishable but for the color of their clothing. The three men soon picked up on her strange behavior. Ten also began looking between the two men—this time both eyebrows went up.

"Great, there are two of you—that's all I need."

Lord Kalil's eyes widened and he pointed to St. Abyn. "But you're…"

"I am the regional Prince of Thieves for the Aquarian sector, with authority to pass through all the portals save the One. How did you find us? How did you get here?"

"You have Authority? But I have Authority! And I am the Sheik of Araby. I outrank you!"

"That's not possible! The portal database only allows one instance of an individual to move between worlds—everybody knows that!"

The two men were now eyeball to eyeball and the level of their voices rose with each exchange.

Ten stepped forward and, putting a firm hand on the nearest shoulder of each, pushed them a few feet apart. "Why don't the two of you show me your IDs?" St. Abyn and Kalil reached into their pockets and grudgingly handed over small circles of silvery material. Ten popped each one into a small device and scanned the readout. "Genetically… you are identical, but… the system does not indicate that you are doppelgangers. The system has not been compromised."

"How else could we be genetically identical? I have seen myself and I am he. This can not be a good thing!" St. Abyn was clearly not happy with how the universe was evolving.

"I don't know. But both of you have been soul tested. You both passed and received Authority. I suggest we figure it out later. We have other things to worry about first." With that, Ten cast his glance toward Amy with a raised eyebrow.

"I'm not a dumb child, you know. I'm perfectly aware that

you are talking about me and would appreciate you addressing some of my questions before we proceed with this quest for whatever it is!" Amy turned her back on the group and began folding up her blanket. She was not going to think about how she had woken up. Or what he must think of her now. She was not.

Kalil stepped forward and raised Amy's hand to his lips. "Ah, yes, my dove, I came to rescue you. I did not want you to be captured by some migrating herdsmen. You would do best to come with me and learn how to make pastries."

Not completely immune to his charm but under no illusions, Amy withdrew her hand, saying, "Thank you very much, but I don't need rescuing. Apparently I am some sort of princess or other. I had best find out about that before returning to England, but then I am going home!"

"But where did you come from, my sweet? My men escorted you from the portal. How did you end up in Araby if that was not your destination?"

Amy looked down at the ground and fiddled with her hair. She did not at all understand how these portal things were working.

St. Abyn coughed politely before saying, "If I may interrupt, it might help to know that she is a Nisqually and unaware of what that means. She has apparently been sequestered in Regency England her entire life. She is not, um, a normal traveler."

"Nisqually!" Kalil breathed in wonder. "But—"

"Exactly. That is what we are going to find out. Care to join us?"

"Find out what?" Amy screeched with perfectly justifiable feminine outrage.

As if by unanimous consent, the men ignored her. As though he had been a member of their party all along, Lord Kalil helped pack up the camp while Amy stood by, clutching her folded blanket. When exactly had she lost control of her own adventure? She thought back and with a resigned sigh decided she probably never had been in charge. The next thing she knew, the men had headed out of the clearing in a single file and she had to run to catch up. St. Abyn graciously gave way to her, and the tiny group proceeded with Ten in the lead and St. Abyn bringing up the rear.

The sunlight filtering through the trees was slightly bluish in color, giving the otherwise unremarkable forest a fae look. There was no clear trail, but Ten strode confidently forward as if there was a path only he could see. The rest of the group followed behind. If they had questions about where they were going, they kept it to themselves, concentrating on not tripping over tree roots as we went. Amy wished she could slow down and explore; everything was so different and intriguing. She wasn't sure if she should be grateful or angry that Ten was acting as though this morning had never happened. Then she started worrying about the next night.

The dense forest gradually gave way to scrubby grasslands. Small- and medium-sized rustles had Amy swiveling her head to try and see the source through the undergrowth. There was a well-trodden path now that they followed, passing tilled fields and distant farmhouses. The little houses all had blue tile roofs that sparkled in the sun. Odd six-legged beasts pulled the otherwise ordinary farm equipment. Occasionally a farmer would wave and Ten would gesture back. They kept moving.

They paused briefly at midday for a cold lunch of leftover beans then were quickly on their way again. The temperature never seemed to waver from a perfect utopian degree, neither too warm nor too cold, and with a slight frisky breeze. The path evolved into a dirt road with deep wheel ruts. Then the shadows began to lengthen again just as a big building near the road came into view.

When they got closer, it became clear it was actually an odd conglomeration of buildings, as though someone had been given a set of life-size building blocks. The entire complex was mud-colored, with slightly lighter thatching for the roof. There were a few stable boys moving horses about in the central courtyard, but the figure that drew everyone's attention was the one that stood completely still and out of the way of traffic where the central building joined the stables.

The Power of Feng Shui

Unmoving in the shadow of the building, the old man was visibly stooped with age. He was wearing rather startling long lavender robes that swathed his body while leaving one blue-veined scrawny shoulder bare. Sparse gray hair radiated out from his head like bird down. With one hand he leaned on a staff taller than he was, while the other held a small circular device with many tiny demarcations around an even smaller central well that held a gyrating metal point. He bowed his head slightly as the group approached.

"Welcome. I am Master An. The swirling chi has hinted of your arrival and the difficult journey ahead. Come in and have some tea." He gestured with his bare arm toward the open door of the inn. Amy, who was by now suffering from a severe case of culture shock, perked up at the familiar mention of tea and moved eagerly toward him and the common room beyond.

"You knew we were coming?" Lord Kalil inquired as the first one to reach the odd old gentleman.

"Oh, yes. There have been troubling things showing up in the north area for months now. Each time I fix them, something new pops up. Clearly travel and strangers are paired. This inn is exactly placed on the slope between the Dragon and the Tiger hills, so I knew you would be passing this way. I have been waiting here for ten years." This last was said with a slight hint of reproach.

Amy hesitated at the threshold of the inn, not sure she wanted to venture into the dark room beyond without backup. Lord Kalil appeared disinclined to just accept the old man's assurances. Perhaps he wasn't quite as easygoing as he'd appeared...

"What exactly are you a master of?" Ten asked even more suspiciously as he drew even with the old man.

"I am a traveling wizard of feng shui."

"Which means what, exactly?" The clipped tone of his voice indicated to everyone that Ten wasn't now nor ever likely to be a practitioner of the art.

"The art and magic of the world's energy in relation to the objects in it." Master An showed no signs of impatience with Ten's attitude, remaining enigmatic. "You, for example, appear to have neglected the southwest corner of your home. Hang a picture of two rabbits there and you will soon see improvements in your love life."

"Not in this lifetime," Ten muttered under his breath. "What do you know about the rabbits? Did they send you?" He leaned, imposing, over the old man, who just gaped at him in confusion.

St. Abyn had to pull hard on Ten's elbow before he would step back. Master An smoothed his robes down before continuing. "You can always use cranes if you feel that strongly about it— and no, I don't know any rabbits personally. They are not native to this planet." He sounded a little confused as to why he was even discussing rabbits he may or may not know.

Amy was puzzled as well. Rabbits were cute and all, and she

wasn't likely to object to a nice rabbit ragout, but she'd never thought to list them in her acquaintance. Clearly a calming cup of tea was needed all round.

By the time she'd turned back toward the door, St. Abyn was already negotiating with the innkeeper at the bar. He turned around as the rest of the group entered the darkly paneled room, a sour expression on his face. "There aren't enough rooms for everyone. There is a small one for Amy on the third floor and one on the second floor that the three of us will have to share."

Master An stepped forward, shaking his head. "Oh no, that will never do. There is stagnant chi on the third floor. Very bad for Miss Amy."

Everyone's eyebrows went up. Ten looked disgusted, St. Abyn and Lord Kalil appeared intrigued, and Amy was just plain worried. She spoke up: "What exactly is stagnant chi? Have the rooms not been properly aired?"

"Child, it is not that simple. The dragon's breath has not been allowed to circulate and is blocked, becoming a force of evil and unbalance. I have been waiting here for you for many years. It is my sacred honor and duty to protect Miss Amy from the evil forces gathering against her." Master An smiled gently as he spoke.

"What evil forces?" Lord Kalil looked over his left shoulder and then his right, as if expecting to see them in the room.

"There are many, but those that are most imminent are the forces of the Originists. They have spies that work with the system. By now they know that one of the royal blood has activated a portal. Their assassins will be here in a few days. It is too dangerous to lose your advantage with such a risk. At best you would not sleep well, at worst…"

Now Amy was near panic and looked helplessly at the other

three men. She did not want to be up on the third floor by herself but was not quite brazen enough to invite herself into the other bedroom. The ebullient Lord Kalil took pity on her.

Slinging a friendly arm around St. Abyn, he said, "Aimee, we would be honored if you would take the bed in our room. We will sleep in front of the door to protect you against all comers!" He raised his hand as though it held a mighty sword and seemed quite cheerful at the thought of battle. Even though a thief, St. Abyn was too much of a gentleman to disagree, but looked slightly perturbed at giving up a perfectly good bed that was plenty big enough for everyone. Amy replied to this offer with graciousness, glad to be away from the bad chi before it could wreak havoc, but secretly disappointed that Ten had not stepped forward to make the offer. She peeked up through her lashes and saw that he was scowling with a certain measure of ferocity. She felt better.

Master An spoke again in his oddly gentle voice: "If none of you object, I will depart with you in the morning. It would be a great honor to lend whatever small talents I possess to assist Miss Amy on her quest."

All the members of the party, with the notable exception of Ten, who just sighed and rolled his eyes, nodded agreeably and gladly accepted the old man into the rapidly growing group.

Local patrons were beginning to arrive in the tap room/reception area for an evening's drinking, so the new comrades moved out of the way. They found a large table at the back of the room and were soon digging into big bowls of stew. After brief introductions (the chi had not passed on actual names of all involved), Master An had quietly excused himself, claiming a need to go over his supplies before they left in the morning.

Amy was seated in a deep booth against the wall between Ten

and Lord Kalil. Not used to drinking alcohol on a daily basis and certainly not at the end of a strenuous day, her single mug of ale quickly went to her head. She found herself nodding forward and jerking back up with her eyes closed.

A while after one such unplanned lurch, she opened her eyes to a field of khaki-green shirt. Taking stock of the situation without moving, she realized she was curled into Ten's broad shoulder with her cheek pressed against his chest. As an embarrassing blush once again began to rise, she heard Lord Kalil's voice as if from a great distance and sounding mournful.

"Once again, I have lost the beautiful girl to another! Will I never find my princess of pastries? It is very sad."

Amy felt the muscled surface beneath her cheek move with laughter.

"I don't think you missed much. This one definitely can't cook."

"Ohhhh!" Outrage replacing embarrassment, Amy sat up and rubbed her face, feeling the fabric creases in her cheeks. She glared at Ten without impact.

"Awake, are you? About time. I don't want to try carrying you up those stairs, and it's time we hit the sack."

"Hit the what?" Lord Kalil interjected.

"Go to sleep."

"Oh, hmm. I like it. 'We should hit the sack.' 'Would you like to hit the sack?' How charming!"

Now Ten was the one glaring. Muttering under his breath, he edged out from the table and stood up. Not unkindly, he gave Amy a hand up and guided her to a standing position, his arm curled around her waist as though he didn't trust her to stay upright without it.

"Sooo," she said quietly, "where are you all sleeping?"

"We are all sleeping in the one room. I hate bedmates so will be sleeping on the floor. The three of you can arm-wrestle for the bed for all I care."

Amy took a step back and tried to hold back the tears perking at the corners of her eyes at this callous attitude. Lord Kalil quickly reiterated his gallant offer from early in the evening, which was echoed by St. Abyn (after a quick elbow in the ribs) as the foursome headed up the stairs. There was an odd lull in the tavern as they departed that did not go unnoticed by the men. Amy, too tired to pick up on anything, headed up the narrow curved stairs and into the bedchamber at the end of the small hall. It was a small square room with rather neat linen-fold paneling on the interior three walls. A single casement window on the outer wall looked out over the back garden. A narrow four-poster bed took pride of place in the center of the room. There was no way that bed could ever be imagined to hold three adults. Simple patchwork quilts covered it, giving it a slightly Bohemian flare. A chest of drawers and a dressing table made up the rest of the furnishings. It was rustic at best. Looking for and not finding water to wash her face, Amy glanced mournfully about, standing in the middle of the room on a multicolored braided rug with her hands at her sides, not quite knowing how to proceed and desperately needing sleep.

"Oh, all right," Ten muttered, taking the not-very-subtle hint. "Anything to get to sleep!" He headed back down the stairs. He returned a few minutes later with a pitcher full of lukewarm water. Amy smiled at him with gratitude. An odd, arrested expression crossed his face. It was the first time he had seen her with a genuine smile, which radiated out of her violet eyes with an amazing effect. Reaching to take the pitcher from Ten, her hands brushed his, which suddenly seemed reluctant to let go of the otherwise ordinary white stoneware vessel. His gaze was locked on Amy's face.

The two other men were poking each other and grinning at the side of the room like a bad Greek chorus in an even worse play. "This is going to be fun!" chimed St. Abyn softly. As Amy reached for a cloth and began dipping it in the water, he reached for the packs they had deposited in the room earlier and began laying out the bedrolls. Ten stood rooted to the spot in the middle of the room, staring at her until Amy, confused by the force of his gaze, turned away to finish washing her face. Then, with a muttered curse, he abruptly headed for the far corner and began sorting through the packs. Dropping her slippers at the side of the bed but still dressed in what had become her nightdress in Lord Kalil's camp, Amy crawled under the covers of the bed, lying as flat and still as possible. St. Abyn and Lord Kalil were already feigning sleep on their respective bedrolls as Ten crossed to the door, moved the dresser in front of it to bar any unwanted visitors, and blew out the candle.

Amy lay in the darkness listening to the strange sounds trickling up from the bar below and wondering how she would ever sleep with all the odd things that had happened in the last two weeks. At least this time she had a warm bed, making it considerably less likely she was going to wake up in a compromising position. She really, really hoped not, anyway. As the men's breathing grew slow and heavy, her eyelids drifted shut.

11

Avoiding the Enemy

Amy's eyes flew open in the darkness when a large hand landed firmly over her mouth. Managing only a muffled "Oommphhh!" she struggled to get her hands up and out from under the covers. Ten's voice was so low as to be barely audible as he whispered in her ear to be very, very quiet. As her immediate panic subsided, to be replaced by another one at this unnamed new threat, she threw back the covers, and after he pushed her to the right she made her way in the darkness to the corner by the window where one of the other two men (how could she tell which one in the darkness?) reached out to take her hand and lead her over to the casement window, which was hanging wide open. A rope was quickly tied around her waist and then the hands placed her hands over the rope just below the knot that anchored it to the window frame. The same hands picked her up and dropped her over the other side of the window.

Willing herself not to scream, Amy came fully awake at this point and, feeling her way down the rope, managed to lower herself to the ground without further sound. She had some experience in daring window escapes at Miss Marchant's Academy, so she wasn't a complete novice. As she neared the bottom, hands reached up and helped her down, quickly untying the rope, which was just as quickly drawn back up out of sight. The moonlight flashed off the white tunic of Lord Kalil as he led her to a horse. Master An was already sitting on a placid little donkey that didn't look like it could escape anything. As he lifted her onto the horse, St. Abyn appeared at her other knee, looked her over, and then quickly led two other horses out of the stable enclosure.

She was dying to ask questions, to know precisely what required their hasty departure without use of the stairs. But all in all she was a sensible young woman and knew that she stood a better chance of getting answers once they were safely away, so she demonstrated her growing maturity and worldly knowledge by simply gathering the reins in her hands and turning the horse toward the road. Ten was the last one down the rope, executing some fancy maneuver that allowed him to unfasten it and coil it up again for future use once he reached the ground. After quickly placing it the saddlebag of the last horse, he gestured to the others to start moving down the road.

Once Ten was in his saddle, Master An wheeled the little donkey around the group, waving his staff in an intricate pattern while chanting. Through the darkness, Amy imagined that she saw a light lavender glow follow the staff through the cool night air. Then, without a word, Ten led the group out of the stable yard and down the road. Master An brought up the rear, periodically turning around and waving his staff some more. The donkey barely seemed awake, but somehow stayed with the group of longer-legged horses without effort.

As the skies began to lighten, Amy started to feel hungry and wondered if it was safe to ask about breakfast. She glanced around at the others and saw Master An breaking from the rear and coming forward. He spoke softly to Ten on her left, who nodded and slowed down, scanning the sides of the road carefully as they rode. She tried to follow his gaze and see what he was seeing, but couldn't imagine what could be capturing his interest so. Then, with a sudden, sharp movement, Ten halted his mount and the other horses, sensing his silent command, halted too without waiting for their riders, who had to work not to fall off. Without speaking, Ten pointed into the trees on the right side of the road, turned his horse, and headed through the underbrush at the roadside and into the trees. Shrugging, Amy and the others followed. About twenty minutes' ride through the forest on no discernible trail, they came to a small clearing, where Ten had already partially set up camp. Amy wondered if he had some secret magic powers that he used when nobody was looking to get there so fast. He looked up from the packs with one raised eyebrow as they dismounted and started talking at once.

"Where are we?"

"What happened?"

"How long are we staying here?"

Ten just raised his other eyebrow at Master An and went back to the pack.

Master An, carefully removing the halter from the donkey, turned to the group. "I was alerted by the shift in energy that the first of the enemies had arrived last night. I alerted your friend here and we planned the escape. I believe I have laid an illusion that will confuse them for a while as to our direction, but we should not tempt fate by being in plain sight on the road in daylight. Their reinforcements will be traveling down that road at any time. I suggest that we rest and catch up on sleep here for the day and continue when night falls."

"But… but what about the harblob?" Amy asked with trepidation and a fair amount of logic.

Master An's eyes widened and he sat up straighter. "I forgot about those. I don't get out much anymore, you see."

Ten looked around the clearing with an air of expertise and authority. "We should be safe enough here. There's no water and low vegetation. Just the same, we'll take turns at watch, with the exception of Master An and Amy."

He began moving rocks and fallen branches until a fire ring was assembled in the center of the clearing. The rest of the group milled around, a little uncertain as to what needed doing. Blowing gently on the infant flames in the campfire, Ten glanced around the group with a bored expression. He hadn't offered up any opinions to anyone about anything, yet Amy got the impression that he was wound tight with anticipation. But for what?

Amy wandered closer to Ten and asked quietly, "You appear to have changed your opinion of Master An?"

Ten's eyes narrowed as he replied with a chagrined tone, "I was convinced by the appearance of an assassin with a very long knife."

St. Abyn had wandered up behind Amy and joined the conversation: "And you are sure he is not in league with them?"

Ten was out of patience. "I have some skills of my own, you know. And one of those happens to have been learned on Omega IX." With a meaningful look at St. Abyn, Ten turned away and began opening cans of beans.

St. Abyn sat back hard on his heels in shock. Amy glanced at him inquiringly. "What is Omega IX? What is he talking about?"

"He means he can read your mind, or rather your intentions,

so be careful what you dream about tonight, eh?" St. Abyn sounded pretty upset.

Amy was bemused, catching the gist of what he'd said but not the literal meaning. How could Ten read minds? But he seemed very confident about Master An, who really was like a kindly, oddly dressed grandfather. Surely that was all he'd meant? That one got a good feeling about Master An?

Amy turned slowly back toward the fire, trying to work all this new information out, only to notice Ten gazing at her stonily from his crouched position by the pan of beans. There were streaks of dirt down the sides of his face, which rather than making him look like an uncouth farmhand served the purpose of outlining his chiseled cheekbones. Amy blamed the fire for the sudden warmth in her cheeks. Evidently Ten wasn't using his mind-reading skills at that very moment, because he stood up and, breaking his gaze from hers, turned to his pack nearby, pulling out the white bed sheet from the inn. Holding it loosely gathered between both hands, he walked toward Amy and unceremoniously began draping it around her, tying the ends in a knot at her shoulder. Shocked into silence to feel his hands about her person like that, Amy finally managed to get a sputter out, only to be stopped by a stony green look.

"This world and the next are considerably more conservative than the last, despite what you may think. You can't go around in that filmy thing without attracting the wrong kind of attention. We'll find you some real clothes when we get to a market."

Without another word, he returned to the beans, looking like he didn't have a care in the world. Amy stood rooted in the spot until Master An approached and began discussing the finer points of sleep direction with her. Grateful for the distraction, she learned quite a bit about feng shui in the next half-hour and even began considering how she could apply it to Riparian Hall.

As the little group gathered around the fire to eat the beans Ten dished out, the conversation turned to the dangers ahead.

"The Originists are on our trail, just as Master An predicted, so we must access the locked portal before they can set a guard or destroy it. If they were to follow us through I don't know what would happen—nobody knows the status of the lost world except to verify that there are no sentient life forms present." St. Abyn always enjoyed the chance to be center stage, something that rarely came to the successful thief.

"Where is the locked portal?" asked Amy with some asperity. She was getting a little tired of wearing the same clothes and not having a hairbrush. If she were in charge of this adventure it would be better provisioned.

St. Abyn continued cheerfully, "Why, it's on your world, so that should be some comfort. In a sense you're going home—just not to the same timeframe."

"Pardon?"

"The portal is known to be present in New York 2020 to 2050. It could be there a few years earlier, and who knows how much further into the future, but those are the dates we have confident verification for."

"2020? But that's—"

"Exactly—a couple hundred years ahead of what you know and on a different continent, so maybe it won't feel quite like home after all. But no matter—it's where we need to head to complete this mission."

Amy didn't have a good argument, but she felt like she ought to. She scrubbed off her tin plate with some nearby leaves and set it aside for someone else to pack. She was getting frustrated with being meek out of ignorance. She gritted her teeth and reached for her bedroll like a seasoned pioneer. Maybe she could catch a quick nap before it was time to resume the journey.

Lord Kalil looked up from his repacking across the fire and asked the group, "So, how do we get to this New York? I don't know that one."

Ten answered without looking up from the fire he was poking. "We have to take the northern portal here to the Wastelands and then from there to the main station on Altaire. That will have a connection to the New York we're seeking. It's not a popular destination, so getting there is a little obscure. No doubt why they chose it to store the locked portal."

The meal and cleanup over, everyone was sitting around the fire. Occasionally someone would make an idle comment that might or might not get a response, but that was about it. Then St. Abyn became very animated and excitedly reached into the depths of his pack and pulled out a small pamphlet. He leafed through it a bit and then got up and started circling the clearing, looking up in the trees as he did so.

"Ah-ha!"

The rest of the group looked up at this but didn't seem inclined to actually move. St. Abyn didn't seem fazed by this obvious lack of enthusiasm. "Come take a look at this!" He gestured to the group at large. Amy decided that if she were first on the scene she was less likely to be out of the conversational loop, so got up off her pallet to go see. Lord Kalil followed shortly behind her.

When they arrived at St. Abyn's location under a fringy pale blue tree, he gestured up on the trunk. "See that number there?"

"The one that says thirty-seven?" Amy responded doubtfully.

"Yes. See here in the guidebook? Thirty-seven corresponds to three and a half stars out of five for questing success and comfort. It says few enemies venture this far off the road, but the lack of amenities means you'd better have brought enough provisions for all members of your party."

Lord Kalil reached out for the pamphlet to take a look. Amy read the cover over his shoulder. In bright blue letters it proclaimed "The Universal Guide to Quest Campsites On Chichen." In smaller gold letters written at an angle were the words "Best Selling Across All Time Dimensions!"

They wandered back toward the fire with Lord Kalil reading out the interesting passages. He found number fifteen had a hot spring for bathing. "Ooh ninety-eight is near a dragon's lair, but it only has two stars," he ended sadly. "Wherever did you get this?"

"It was on the front desk at the inn. I helped myself to it to see if it would be useful. We left in such a hurry I didn't have time to look through it until now."

"If there's a guidebook, why have we been wandering about so much?" Amy inquired. At this point they were back with Ten and Master An. Ten stood up to see what had their attention and then blinked three times at the sight of the book. Without a word, he removed it from Lord Kalil's hands and flipped through it. Amy thought she heard a barely audible "shit," but that was his only verbal reaction. He flipped back to where a map was located, studied it for several minutes as though committing it to memory, and then handed the thin book back without a word. He turned away and began rearranging his pack for the tenth time that day.

When dusk fell, the whole group began packing up without talking. Loads were redistributed on the horses for better

balance, and Lord Kalil gave Amy a leg up on her horse. Master
An seemed to float onto the back of the little donkey at the
front of the parade, and then they were moving back toward
the road.

That night's ride was relatively uneventful. Unidentified night
creatures commented on their presence with soft whistles and
barks but did not approach. They took turns riding lead and
last, and those that rode in the rear reported feeling watched.
Master An and his little donkey, named Shameless—as the
group soon learned, for her endless begging—were enveloped
in a lavender mist that glowed just enough to light the way
ahead. Amy's eyes were drooping with the strain of trying to
see into the dark when the group finally halted, seemingly in
the middle of nowhere. Still mounted, St. Abyn and Ten were
talking quietly to the side. Ten gestured Lord Kalil forward and
spoke quietly. When they separated, Lord Kalil turned back
to Amy and Master An, gesturing them off the road while the
other two turned back the way they had come.

"Hurry, Aimee. We must take cover."

"But where are they going? Are they leaving us? Why are they
going back?"

"They have some shopping to do. Hurry now through these
bushes and then we will have to dismount to reach the shelter."

"Shopping! But that's my forte." Amy made to turn her horse
around, but despite his nonchalance, Lord Kalil was faster,
grabbing her mount's bridle.

"Shopping is a bit of a… how do you say it? Euphemism.
Best not to ask too many questions. Come now and let's show
them how your cooking skills have improved, yes?"

Amy glared at him but acquiesced, at least in terms of their
travel direction. She did help find fallen branches in the little

clearing, nearly identical to the one they had left as night fell, but somehow the cooking fell to Master An. Not a bean aficionado, he soon had a small pot of stew bubbling on the edge of the fire.

He and Amy walked a circle around the clearing, looking up into the trees, but try as they might they couldn't see any numbers. Amy was disappointed. She wanted to know what others thought about this particular campsite and whether there were some nearby attractions they could visit.

12

More Bad Guys

Ten and St. Abyn returned to the campsite just as Master An was dishing up the stew. They tended the horses before sitting down on the fallen logs Lord Kalil had arranged in a semicircle in front of the fire. Ten grimaced slightly at the sight of the stew but ate it without complaining. When everyone was done and the dishes tucked back away, the two men unloaded their packs. Foodstuffs were laid out, examined, and sorted to be repacked with their existing supplies.

Ten handed Amy a stack of clothing. "These should fit well enough. You'll need to be able to move and not draw attention where we're going."

"But they're... brown." She made a moue of distaste.

"Exactly."

"Just a minute." She remembered Lord Kalil's earlier comment. "Are these stolen?"

"Technically, yes, as we didn't ask permission. But before you go off in a huff, we left some money for what we took. We can't draw attention to ourselves in any way. Someone is trying to kill you, remember?"

He pushed the clothes at her again, and this time she took them. She realized she couldn't go anywhere to change (the harblob, remember?), but she decided that the sheet Ten had draped around her earlier would do in a pinch. So with much wriggling and gasping, she managed to shed the silk shift and put on the new shirt and trousers without too much incident. He had even found her a pair of stout boots that were just a little big in the toes so she could finally shed her worn-out slippers. She folded up the now dirt-streaked sheet as best she could and then stretched her legs out in front of the fire to admire her boots.

"We looked but we couldn't find a campsite number for this place to look it up in the guidebook. Do you know what it is?"

"It doesn't have one, that's why we stopped at this one. The last thing we need is to be running into other travelers or assassins masquerading as travelers. I picked one that wasn't on that damn guidebook map."

"Oh."

Amy couldn't help but be disappointed. Without a guidebook to draw attention to the special features of this campsite, she didn't see how she was supposed to distinguish it from the one last night or the one tomorrow. They all looked the same and they did pretty much the same things in each one. A numbering system made sense. But apparently Ten was not a fan of that much social validation.

Lord Kalil perched himself next to Ten, who had signaled he'd take the first watch.

"What if the portal in New York isn't accessible?"

"Then we'll have to divert to the one on that swamp world. It's going to have to be a last resort, though—it's infested with exiled assassins."

Matching expressions of distaste appeared on the faces of the Lord Kalil and St. Abyn, distracting Ten for a second, his eyes narrowing, but he said nothing. "It will work," declared Lord Kalil. "The gods will put many obstacles in our path, but even they would not ask me to enter a swamp!"

"It's a three-day ride to the transport that we need to New York. We'd better take stock of our supplies and weapons before we reach the edge of the Aasland Plains."

As dawn began to lighten the sky, they spread their blankets around the dying fire. Amy wondered if she was ever going to see anything of this world besides forest clearings. Without thinking about it, she found she had placed her blanket next to Ten's, but when she peeked at him his back was to her. She tried not to feel hurt that he always seemed so distant, and turned to her other side.

Late that afternoon, when she thought they would be heading out again, she learned that no, they would be staying through another night and tomorrow heading out at daybreak. They did a full inventory of their packs (again) and Ten and St. Abyn disappeared on yet another shopping expedition. This time in a slightly different direction. When they returned, Amy couldn't see that they'd obtained anything, but both men wore a satisfied expression.

Ten showed them a deep, spring-fed pool in a little rock-walled glade just beyond the clearing, so they each took time to clean up. Amy washed her hair using soapweed she found nearby as shampoo. She hurried because Ten was standing guard on the other side of the rock formation and she didn't want to take the chance that he would feel the need to come around to investigate some strange sound. But that didn't stop her from writing a mental guidebook review in her head. Personally, this chance to get clean definitely raised this campsite up to five stars. She began to wonder what other travelers did on their quests. Surely they weren't all trying to get to the Lost City. Maybe she could find some that were going to go exploring on other worlds and join them once she'd done her "key" thing.

Feeling much better, she re-dressed in her new brown outfit. "Ten? I'm ready," she called out as she sat on a nearby boulder and tried to finger-comb her hair. He sauntered out from behind the back wall of the grotto, his expression rather intentionally blank.

"You don't happen to have a comb, do you?"

He fingered his close-cropped hair. "Uh, no—never really have the need of one."

Amy sighed heavily. It was now or never.

"How come you don't like me?"

"What makes you say that?" He sounded genuinely surprised.

"You never really talk to me. And… and…"

"And?"

"Twice now I've ended up draped all over you and you just set me aside like an old pair of gloves." She looked down at her feet, her face hot. "That's it, isn't it? I'm a wanton hussy and you don't want anything to do with me." The tears were beginning to gather behind her eyes for an all-out assault.

Ten's jaw dropped and he raked a hand through his hair, this time in frustration. "Amy…"

"What?"

Her wet hair had fallen forward, obscuring her face from view.

He walked over and pulled her up with a large hand under her elbow. She rose reluctantly but kept her eyes on the toes of his boots. She sniffled back the tears. His other hand rose to draw the hair back from her face. "Oh, Amy," he sighed, and with that he leaned in and gently placed his mouth over hers.

Her arms crept up of their own volition to his shoulders.

"Yep, you're a hussy, all right."

Amy didn't miss the note of laughter in his voice but was too thrilled with this development to call attention to it. This felt like what she'd been waiting for the last few years. Shivers of excitement tingled down her spine.

He pulled her closer, and as her arms embraced the steel of his back, his hands cradled her face. He gave her one more soft kiss. His voice was tinged with regret that she didn't understand. "Amy, I know all this is new to you, but you need to understand. For ten years I've been preparing for the ultimate mission. When I was charged with it I was told there was no way out, but that my ultimate sacrifice would be much appreciated." He stepped back from her to rake his hand through his hair again. She was beginning to see this as something of a nervous habit.

"But you don't have to do it, surely? We could find someone else?"

He smiled without humor. "It doesn't really work that way. These orders didn't come from a human government. There are… beings that supervise. They're the ones that contacted me. And that night… that night their minions did things to me. I couldn't back out if I wanted to."

"What did they do to you?" she whispered.

He touched her cheek softly with his fingers. "Nothing you should hear about. The point is that I don't expect to survive this. What I'm hoping for is to make sure you're safe so at least it won't be a wasted effort. Understand?"

Amy did, but she wasn't in agreement. It seemed to her that he'd accepted this fate without much of an attempt to find an alternative. She wasn't prepared to let him go that easily.

She narrowed her eyes at him. "And if you don't die?"

He smiled and gave her a perfunctory kiss on the forehead. "Then I will do my best to ensure that you never get the chance to drape yourself over any other man."

He still didn't sound like he thought that would happen, so Amy decided she would just have to figure something out. She took the hand he held out to her and they headed back to camp.

When they got back, Master An was walking the compass points of their little clearing, but other than feng shui Amy hadn't discovered that he had too much else to talk about. He was kindly, though, so she spent a few minutes in conversation just to be polite.

St. Abyn was in charge of dinner, and with the newly liberated foodstuffs managed to whip up eggs and sausages, a heavenly reprieve from beans and stew. Right there Amy felt that this campsite was one of great distinction, head and shoulders above the others that were in the guidebook. Amy sat down next to Ten with her metal plate and tried to get him to talk about himself, but despite their earlier conversation he didn't respond to any of the social niceties she'd been taught. She gave up and started counting the emerging stars instead. The constellations were completely different. She wished she had a notebook so she could do some notations and sketches.

The next day, they packed up the horses and headed out at first light. Within an hour they had passed the last bit of civilization and were clearly in the wild lands. The scenery went unchanged for miles after that, and since the horses were doing all the work, Amy let her mind drift. What kind of princess was she? Did it come with a tiara she could wear to the assemblies? Perhaps a clothing allowance? She tried to picture Ten in formal dress and failed miserably. She didn't think her future powers would extend to that much coercion anyway.

When the sun was high in the sky and there was no breeze to disperse the heat, they reached the Aasland Plains. An enormous dry floodplain, there was no cover of any kind. Scrubby grass grew in patches, but that was about it. Ten signaled them to pick up the pace, and the horses didn't seem inclined to argue. Amy shifted her shoulders, trying to move the hot spots that were getting more than uncomfortable. The chatter in the group had died down hours ago; now each member was focused on the horse ahead and on simply getting through the day and out of the open. Despite their attention to the danger and the omnipresent itch between shoulder blades, there was no warning when the sky went dark with hurtling figures that were screeching with rage. As they descended toward the travelers, the group gasped and frantically reached for whatever weapon was at hand.

They were horrible creatures, an odd and repulsive mixture of fantasy and reality, animal and human. A winsome woman's mouth was paired with the vacant eyes of a zombie swamp mole. They all had hideously fetid breath that seemed to suck the very life out of the small group. Ten and St. Abyn were both wheeling their horses continuously and using a combination of handheld and throwing knives to fend off the closest beasts. Lord Kalil slashed at the rest with a nasty-looking curved sword that appeared seemingly out of nowhere, and Amy did her best to contribute by grasping her staff firmly in both hands and bashing at anything that got within striking range. Meanwhile, Master An was frantically consulting his compass and then perusing the landscape. Finally he gestured to the right. "Quickly, that way! There is a white tiger hill beyond the turtle mound." A screeching flying creature did a kamikaze run over their heads, laughing with a young girl's giggle while it did so.

The group struggled to move toward the hill, holding their breath, and continued swatting the beasts out of the way. Almost overcome with the smell, Amy let her guard down for a single second and one particularly ugly specimen swooped in and grasped her shoulder. Amy screamed with pain and fright. Ten jerked around, and in a single motion skewered it and flung it away. Rivulets of blood ran down Amy's arm. As their group passed over the low mound, the creatures gave way slightly. Master An waved his hands in a complicated figure that was not quite visible. With a shaking of the earth, the hill in front of them erupted. Bits of earth with grass attached slid over the flanks of an enormous white tiger. It left the ground, leaping over the small group as though it were unaware of their existence. Immediately its attention focused on the menagerie of creatures in the air. The tiger flung back its head then lowered it again while flame burst from its mouth. The creatures disappeared with soft pops like bursting soap bubbles.

It was over as quickly as it began. The tiger (the size of a small village) loped off over the mountain range and disappeared. With unspoken unanimous consent, the small band of weary adventurers made their way to the end of the plains, a mere quarter-mile from the battle site, and set up camp in a small grove of rowan trees. There were injuries to tend to, but nobody wanted to be ambushed again, so getting out of the open was the first priority. While Master An and Lord Kalil looked after the horses, Ten drew Amy to her feet, and without a word began pulling her shirt off and away from the wounds on her shoulder. He was reasonably gentle but completely unconcerned for her modesty.

"Ten! What are you doing? Stop it!" She batted at his hands

ineffectively.

"And let you get infected and die at this point? I don't think that would be fair to the rest of us that want to get into that portal." He turned her around again so her back was to him and continued to pull the shirt down her arms. "Behave, and this will be over before you know it." He sound amused, like he was dealing with a small child. But once the masculine shirt was off and only her silk chemise-like garment was keeping her from being naked, his touch changed. He cleaned the wounds efficiently but managed to extend his fingers well beyond the few square inches of her shoulder. Every time she involuntarily twitched in response, his other hand would tickle her waist. She found herself leaning back into his touch and arching her head back to meet his.

"There, all done. That wasn't so painful, now, was it?" There was a world of masculine satisfaction in his amused voice as he released her. Caught off guard and off balance, she stumbled a bit before regaining her equilibrium.

Amy turned around and blushed when she realized that everyone else had stopped their tasks and was standing around the camp area, observing them with a great deal of interest. She saw a gold coin slide from St. Abyn's hand to Lord Kalil's and her temper simmered. She grabbed the shirt Ten had removed from the ground and shoved her arms back in the sleeves. Making sure that each and every member of the party got his fair share of her glare of righteous indignation, she walked over to her saddlebag and began repacking things without actually seeing what it was that she was moving about. Muffled chuckles erupted randomly for the next few minutes while dinner was prepared and the horses watered.

Fresh from his gambling victory, Lord Kalil took pity on her and began telling stories of great derring-do in far-off lands as they gathered near the fire to eat the hastily prepared meal. Night was falling and the shadows highlighted the similarities between the faces of Kalil and St. Abyn. It was an uncanny resemblance. Nobody talked as they lay their beds near the fire in a rough circle. Amy was gently edged in toward the fire so that there were bodies between her and the dark trees. She didn't protest. Tomorrow would be another long day as they made their final leg to the portal. She needed her sleep.

In the morning, there was more upsetting news. Her horse had also been scratched in the creature conflict and would not be able to be saddled. After some guttural comments and hand gestures, her bags were reapportioned to the other horses. Then, with a charming smile and a flourish, St. Abyn lifted her up to the saddle of a waiting horse. Amy grimaced at having to share a ride again after all this, but didn't complain. Waiting to feel St. Abyn come up behind her, she didn't look around until she realized that wasn't happening. Her eyes narrowed when she saw St. Abyn and Lord Kalil already mounted on the two remaining horses, Master An astride his little donkey. "Wha..." was as much as she got out as Ten crossed over to her horse after kicking the dead campfire to ensure it was out. He grinned at her cockily, the first full smile anyone had seen on his face in fifteen years, and swung up behind her.

The others moved their horses out of the trees as Ten lifted Amy up with an iron arm under her ribcage, scooted forward so he was comfortably seated in the saddle, and then set her down again so that she was essentially resting on his thighs. Outraged and slightly intrigued, she whipped her head around and glared. He smiled back at her innocently and gathered up the reins. Afraid to lose her balance, she turned forward again and tried to think of why this was so wrong, illogical, or any other defense. She couldn't come up with much other than it was unladylike. Holding her close with his left hand, Ten guided the horse with his right and pretty soon they were leading the train down the trail toward the portal in the small town of Tuffna.

After about an hour of riding past basically the same scenery, Ten apparently got bored and the fingers on his left hand started to get creative. Granted, there wasn't too much he could do one handed while riding, but he amused himself nonetheless. Amy could feel the burn of eyes focused on the point right at the base of her neck. It took all her will power not to turn around and give him a piece of her mind. After ten minutes of steaming, she suddenly realized that Miss Marchant's Academy had lost its hold on her forever and whipped herself around to glare at her tormentor. Her eyes narrowed to dangerous slits when she saw that Ten was only looking amused, not embarrassed and guilty as she'd hoped.

He looked her in the eye and drawled, "You're looking a little riled up. Is something the matter?"

Ten couldn't know that at that moment he came the closest to death that he ever had (with the exception of the rabbits). He was saved only by the triviality of Amy not wanting to have to go through the whole dismounting and remounting the horse to dispose of the body.

13

Even More Bad News

They arrived at Tuffna, the town with the portal, without further incident. Amy was in an oddly flustered state, and Ten was walking a bit stiffly, but other than that things were fine. None of them had really let down their guard on the remainder of their journey, and there had been frequent stops while Master An consulted his compass, so they all breathed a sigh of relief when the town gates came into view. Tuffna looked like the small fortress town that it was, barricaded within crenellated stone walls with round towers on the corners. People were moving around, but quickly, without stopping to chat out in the open. As the little group on horseback approached the reinforced wooden gates, a guard in heavy armor stepped forward. "Halt, who goes there?"

Ten muttered under his breath to St. Abyn, "Did he really just say that? Nobody really says that!"

Lord Kalil, obviously sensing that Ten wasn't at his most diplomatic (which, let's face it, wasn't a particularly high bar to start with), took the initiative and moved his horse forward a few steps level with the guard. "We are travelers from the north just seeking shelter for the night before we continue our journey."

"The north! Nobody gets through the north pass these days."
The guard's eyes narrowed suspiciously, but he really was more
for show than anything else, so he let them pass with a "See
that you don't cause any trouble."

They rode through the gate and down a narrow street that
opened up into the market square, bustling with the usual
wagons and small stalls selling stuff that nobody ever seemed
to really need. St. Abyn separated from the group and hunted
down a stable that was willing to hold Master An's donkey (for
a fee, of course) and buy the other horses. Nobody said it, but
none of the rest were planning to return to this world ever
again unless they absolutely had to.

Once that transaction was taken care of, St. Abyn returned
to the group and they all went off in search of the portal. St.
Abyn claimed to know the general location, but because the
portals were well hidden and businesses had a way of changing
and remodeling, sometimes things got confusing. This was
one of those times. Having gone around the same block of
buildings at least ten times, everyone was getting impatient.
The shopkeepers were beginning to look at them strangely. St.
Abyn, however, ignored them all and continued to consult his
little pocket device and squint at rooflines while occasionally
tripping over a cobble. Finally he motioned everyone forward
with a wave of his arm and headed into a private house without
knocking on the door first. The lady of which was a rather large
woman kneading what looked like bread dough in the kitchen
they entered directly from the street. Her mouth falling open,
the woman reached for the nearby rolling pin and started
forward. For once in tandem, St. Abyn and Lord Kalil used
their combined charms to great effect:

"My lady! My friend here was overcome with emotion! His

memories of his dear granny in this very kitchen are so strong that he forgot she's been dead and buried these twenty years. Forgive us, do!" She lowered the rolling pin fifteen degrees.

St. Abyn bowed low. "Indeed, mistress! My apologies. Indeed, my granny would give me little apple pies after school in this very room. She made the best apple pie I've ever tasted." This last was a purely calculated move, which worked.

The rolling pin was put down with a "Hummphhhh! We'll just see about that! Sit! Sit! Now you tell me this isn't better pie than your granny made! Won first place in the Aasland Bakeoff of '32." With that, she pushed each one of them into a chair at the rustic table and set a still-steaming apple pie right in the center. She bustled around with plates and silverware, and before anyone could say a word about going upstairs, they had some truly fabulous pie in their mouths.

St. Abyn had no trouble reassuring the waiting haus frau that her pie was indubitably superior. Somewhat mollified, she absolutely beamed when Kalil asked, "Do you by any chance have any single daughters or nieces that can bake like you?" It seemed that she didn't.

St. Abyn sighed slightly and poked Kalil in the ribs unobtrusively before asking, "Madame, I have so many fond memories of this house. Would it be all right if I showed my friends the attic where I used to play?"

"The attic! It's just all cobwebs and such." She was back to being slightly suspicious.

"Ah, but when you're a young boy, cobwebs are the stuff of mystery!"

Reluctantly she assented and waved them toward the back stairs.

Figuring out of sight, out of mind was the way to play this, they hurried single file up the narrow back stairs, down the hall, and up a ladder to the attic hatch. Once they were all standing in the center of the attic, the only place with enough height to accommodate them, they looked around at what was truly an impressive collection of cobwebs. Dust motes glinted in the dim light coming from a dirty round window at one end. Carefully navigating the trunks and broken furniture that was haphazardly arranged, St. Abyn led the way to the back of the room. There, an impossibly large wardrobe dominated the wall. It could never have come up that ladder, Amy remarked to herself. Apparently she was the only one with a practical mind, because nobody else mentioned it. Ten and St. Abyn set to work opening the wardrobe door and fiddling with some controls set behind a sliding panel at the back. Nothing happened. They fiddled some more. Still nothing happened.

Ten grunted as he emerged from an awkward position at the base of the wardrobe. "Let's see if we can shift it out— something seems to be out of whack. The emergency override should have worked."

The three men braced themselves against the sides of the wardrobe while Master An and Amy looked on. With a great deal of grunting, they managed to shift the wardrobe away from the wall a few inches without making too much noise that might alert the woman of the house.

Ten shone his tiny penlight into the gap. "Son of a bitch!"

St. Abyn leaned on Ten's shoulder to take a look, almost knocking him over in the process. "Oh."

"What?" Amy cried with impatience.

Ten sighed as he rose from his crouched position, rubbing his lower back as he did so. "Even portal cables aren't immune from teeth."

"Teeth! Whose teeth?"

St. Abyn, significantly more subdued, responded, "I would guess Rattus Rattus."

Amy put her knowledge of Latin to good use. "A rat! Where?" She started looking frantically around her ankles.

"Long gone, I presume. There's quite a bit of dust on the frayed ends."

"Oh." She too calmed down. "Now what?" she inquired softly.

St Abyn spoke sadly: "We'll have to go over the eastern pass to the other portal. This one is out of commission, unless you happen to have a 3x09ab cable on you somewhere."

Ten waved everyone back to the ladder. "We'd better go find an inn for the night. Nothing more we can do here."

After saying their adieus to the plump lady in the kitchen, who pressed another apple pie on them, they headed back out to the street and the market square. The sun was beginning to fade and lit torches were placed in the wall brackets outside the pubs, and yes, an inn. Lord Kalil took the honors and headed in. A short time later, he emerged dangling a key. "I managed to get the room over the stables." At the resounding groans from everyone else, he frowned. "It's quiet and private with a separate entrance. I too can be practical, you know!" He sounded a bit miffed that his careful planning was going unappreciated.

Amy touched his arm in sympathy. "Well, I think it's an excellent plan, and perhaps one or both of you gentlemen could go get some food from that pub to accompany our pie? And perhaps some ale?" With that, she took Lord Kalil's arm and headed down the narrow passage by the end that led to the stables. Master An, who seemed to always trail behind everyone, followed, gently waving his staff in a loose pattern over their heads. With a raised eyebrow, Ten gestured for St. Abyn to lead the way to the pub.

They had a lovely evening picnic in the stable loft. It was a long room with exposed rafters overhead. Six single beds were lined up along one wall, and a faint but not overwhelming stable odor drifted up through the floorboards. Amy was growing quite a taste for ale and didn't hold back. That contributed in part to the rousing country dance she executed with Lord Kalil, who wanted to demonstrate the superior noise resistance of his room choice. St. Abyn hummed a merry tune as an accompaniment and Master An thumped his staff in time. The only one not participating in some way was Ten, who lay back on his bed and stared at the ceiling, his arms crossed on his chest. When the dance ended and Amy was laughingly about to accept St. Abyn's request for his turn, Ten sat up.

"She's had enough." His intonation left no room for negotiation. The others all frowned at him but he just stood up, took Amy by the hand, and sat her down on the end of the nearest bed. With his constant companion, the penlight, in his hand, he moved her shirt away to check her bandage. Pointing at the small but fresh stain, he repeated, "Enough".

She supposed she had to agree, but it had been fun. A body can only take so much disappointment and misadventure in one day, after all. She smiled at him and kissed him on the cheek, which she was beginning to learn was the best way to unnerve him. Sure enough, a ruddy tide was rising up his face. She laughed outright and bent to take her boots off. She'd decided earlier in the day that if he was suffering from some misplaced sense of nobility she was just going to have to take charge and fix things to her satisfaction.

The next morning, St. Abyn drew a rough map in the dust on the floor. "This is the quickest route from here to there. But this notch here"—he gestured at a point midway—"is known for brigands. They aren't unionized, so I have no influence. If anything, if they knew who I was they'd be looking for ransom."

Ten scrutinized the map for several minutes before nodding. "Let's get going—we need to be past that pass by nightfall."

With that, they all rose and began packing up their gear. Without the horses they would have to go on foot. Buying them back seemed pointless, as apparently much of the way was too hazardous and they would have to be walked anyway. They bought some fresh bread and cheese from one of the market stalls on their way back to the city gate. The morning was warm and sunny, with just a tickle of breeze that stirred the wind chimes by the temple doors.

Once outside the gates, they took the path leading east. It skirted a pastoral lake before quickly climbing toward the pass. Amy readjusted the straps of her pack and looked toward the snow-capped peaks in the distance. "Are we going up there?"

"No, the pass cuts below and to the right. You'll be able to see it in a bit." Ten came up level with her and walked alongside in silence. They stopped for a quick lunch of dried meat and bread at a picnic table that seemed to appear out of nowhere. Its neglect suggested that it had been placed there in happier times. An eagle soared over the valley they had left behind that morning. Amy gazed at it in awe, but Ten and St. Abyn looked at each other with concern. "Time to keep going."

Two hours later, the small band of travelers rounded the curve of the switchback and came out from the trees into a shallow valley dotted with the deep blue of the mimchi flower. The light lemon scent of the small blossoms wafted gently on the breeze. They paused for a second to take in the very normalness of a mountain valley in late spring. Small patches of snow still clung to the shadows, but with the crystalline glare that indicated they would not be able to hold out much longer. The little group began moving again as a single unit without a word being spoken, down the path worn through the tundra and out into the open alpine pasture.

They had progressed about halfway across when the sun reached its apex, glaring through the thin air. A slight breeze danced across the wildflowers and unfurling fronds. The air was cool, but the sun's warmth worked through the many layers and soon they were shedding outer garments and adding them to the already stuffed packs. Settled down into a rhythm of one foot after the other, there was no conversation and all eyes focused on the hills ahead, where the path would lead them back under the trees and toward a final ascent of the mountain.

Without a sound, a shadow swooped across them, the first of the day since entering the valley. The arrows were upon them before their eyes had lifted from the distant horizon.

They all knew they were too far across the meadow to turn back, and yet the only shelter existed in the scrubby trees at the edge, an impossible distance away. They began running anyway, as fast as they could. The packs weighed them down but also provided a small bit of armor against the raining spears.

Amy felt heat bloom in her previously unwounded shoulder and looked to see blood dripping down. Before she could fall, Ten swept her up in his arms and kept running. Amy gritted her teeth to keep from screaming at the wrenching pain each bounce was causing. She tucked her head against his shoulder and urged him on silently.

Suddenly screams erupted overhead, the piercing screech of

an animal in pain and the grinding gears of machinery. Amy risked a glance up and saw an odd winged creature tumbling toward the ground with a feathered spear sticking out of it. The sun caught the metal gears of the creature's breast as it rotated over and under toward its death.

More spears were launched from the trees, which were now visible as individual units that were getting closer, but not fast enough. But the flying death machines had switched their attention from their initial prey and were now circling over the trees, seeking their attackers. The first of the group, Ten carrying Amy, and then St. Abyn reached the underbrush, where unseen hands grabbed them and whisked them farther back and down.

When Amy caught her breath, she realized she was being held down below the branches of an imshu bush, whose wide, leather-like leaves overlapped to create an almost impervious shield. She looked at the impossibly long fingers gently pushing on her shoulder and followed them back to look into elegant, slanted green eyes in a narrow face framed by straight fair hair. Pointed ears parted the hair at the sides. Glowing blue beads were interspersed on narrow braids. Amy's eyes widened at the sight just as the black edges began to encroach on her vision. "Who are you? What are you?"

"I am Syrgnor. We"—he gestured at what Amy could vaguely see was a group of about fifty archers that all looked exactly like him—"are what you might call elves. Naturally, we prefer 'Leanadhe.' Come, let me tend your shoulder." Amy was hardly in a position to protest as he unbuttoned her tunic and moved the tatters out of the way. A barbed arrow fletch stuck into her shoulder. (Somewhat like a meat thermometer in a turkey, an accurate if unflattering image.)

At that moment, Ten walked over. "What the hell do you think you're doing?" he growled.

"Saving her life. Would you prefer I stop?"

Ten groused quietly, but sank down on his heels and took Amy's free hand in his. She gripped it tightly as Syrgnor held her shoulder with one hand and yanked out the arrow with the other. The sudden welling of blood had Ten turning a bit pale and looking away.

The elven healer reached into one of his many pouches and scattered a gold powder over the wound. As he did so, the bleeding slowed and Amy felt the feverish heat begin to dissipate. Another pouch produced a clean white bandage that was wrapped around and under her shoulder, and yet another a potion that was held to her lips. She drank and promptly sank into a deep slumber.

Syrgnor wrapped the bloody arrow in the remains of her tunic and stood. "You might want to find her a clean shirt and then pick her up again. We'll be heading out shortly."

Ten just raised an eyebrow at that.

"You don't think we just hang out here for the fun of it, do you? We had word of your coming and your quest. It is in the best interest of the Leanadhe that balance is restored, and while that may rest in your fair lady's hands, we have ways of assisting that are not otherwise available to you." With that cryptic explanation, Syrgnor headed back to his comrades for a quiet conference.

Ten carried the sleeping Amy back over to St. Abyn and Lord Kalil, both of whom had had their more minor wounds tended to by others and were standing waiting with their packs already on their backs. He was worried about her; she didn't look like she had spare blood to lose and they hadn't even gotten to the really dangerous part of their journey. He pulled her more tightly to him so she wouldn't be jostled. Another of the elves gestured them forward and our heroes were soon surrounded by the archers. They headed deeper into the woods, away from the trail and the path to the portal. Ten didn't see that he had much alternative but to follow, but he was still feeling a bit dubious when the group halted in front of a very large tree indeed. The lead elf placed his hand against the trunk, and with a gentle creaking and stretching, the fibers of the tree trunk moved to the left and the right, leaving a glowing blue door exactly in the middle. With that, an elf took the hand of each one of the humans and led them into the blue tree trunk. Since Ten was still carrying the slumbering Amy, his escort simply took him by the shoulder and nudged him forward.

14

The Land of the Leanadhe

Amy came to while still in Ten's arms as they walked into the tree and entered the land of the Leanadhe. He set her gently on her feet. "How come I'm the one those creatures keep coming after—is it just because they know I'm the least skilled? I'm out of unwounded shoulders."

She felt a rumble coming from deep within him. It emerged as a rusty chuckle. He threw an arm around her waist, careful not to bump her shoulders, and Amy could feel that he was taking some of her weight. She could walk just fine but didn't see a need to complain. Whatever had been in that potion had brought her back almost to normal. They stopped for lunch at the shores of a silver lake. Swans scudded by in full majesty, and Amy was enchanted. When she turned around, another elf had appeared, this one even taller, with pointier ears if that were possible. He bowed low. "My lady, I am Prince Asnyr, at your service. Welcome to our realm. I am glad to see that you and your friends are safe." With that, he proffered an arm, which she accepted out of habit.

A half-hour later, Amy found herself walking down a flower-strewn path still on the arm of the elven prince Asnyr. Glancing down, she discovered that her bloodstained garments had been transformed into an elegant dimity day gown trimmed with sage-green ribbons—just the thing for a walk in the garden. Except that she no longer felt like a young lady of quality wishing for balls and handsome suitors. She was beginning to feel the weight of responsibility and leadership—neither called for dimity. That was not to say she didn't spare a few extra moments to gaze up at the impossibly beautiful profile of her escort. The pointed ears and long blond hair really shouldn't work as well as they did. Asnyr must have felt her gaze, because he glanced down at her while lifting a sardonic eyebrow. Amy moved her gaze back to the scenery quickly. She glanced back over her shoulder to see that the rest of her friends were in the middle of the phalanx of elven archers. Ten was frowning in her direction, but he had no room to maneuver to get any closer. She smiled to herself. Good, let him get a taste of not being in control for once.

While the concept of a flower-strewn meadow was familiar, this particular landscape was like nothing she could have imagined. The delicate trees, not large enough to be imposing but just tall enough to give scale, sported true gold and silver leaves that shimmered in the light breeze. The path appeared to be gravel, but not the usual gray kind—rather, crushed amethysts that glinted and sparkled in the blue light. For overhead was not sky with a sun, but another land surface that was shades of blue, a darker cobalt in the depths that could barely be discerned and a pale icicle blue/white in the stalactites that reached down in gothic tracery. It was like being in a giant landscaped cave, one without discernible sides.

She glanced behind her again for a longer look to see their motley crew had also had a full wardrobe change, although nothing quite as elegant. Master An sported a fresh, unstained lavender robe, the sheik was in clean white trousers and a robe reminiscent of the day they had met, and St. Abyn next to him all in black. Ten was the only one wearing a uniform she didn't recognize. Blotchy green fabric with all sorts of extra pockets and doodads made his already imposing frame seem massive. His expression indicated something was chafing, but she couldn't tell if it was the outfit or their escort. Mixed among the group and stretching as far back as she could see were the elven archers; eerily similar in appearance with slanted green eyes and pale blond hair, they all carried the long bows with the glowing blue beads. Their clothing too had transformed from the forest green and brown tunics to ones that seemed made of silver snakeskin, with seamless black trousers.

Whatever magic had re-dressed everyone had not refreshed them otherwise. There was no chatter, and the humans at least looked tired. Ten was frowning up at the stalactites as though daring them to make a move.

"My lady, our destination approaches." Asnyr spoke softly from her side. Amy peered eagerly into the blue horizon, and just then as they rounded a bend in the path, a fairytale silver castle appeared. Turrets and crenellations crowded the massive roofline and purple pennants flew from every possible point. The flowers grew denser and gradually formed themselves into formal gardens with impossibly elaborate fountains in the centers. They entered the castle's courtyard and Amy was struck by two things: the foundation of the castle was boulders of amethyst crystals, and there was nobody else in sight—no groundskeepers, doormen, or any other laborers of the sort usually required to keep this kind of residence running.

Giant silver doors with engraved gold strap work swung open as the group approached. Asnyr ushered them into the foyer while saying, "Welcome to Caoswythe Palace. My father is honored that you have graced us with your royal presence and your friends. Please make yourselves at home." With that, torches set into the walls and up the grand staircase flared up, illuminating the cavernous entryway. Without conscious direction, Amy felt her feet take her toward the staircase and up then down a long central hall. At the end, double doors swung open of their own accord and she found herself in a charming bedchamber dressed in shades of sapphire blue and silver. Six tall windows overlooked a private courtyard with a rose garden. Too tired to really take it all in, Amy undressed and crawled under the covers. The lights dimmed automatically and she closed her eyes.

15

An Offer of Marriage

In the morning, Amy awoke refreshed and rejuvenated. All her bruises and sore spots from the past several weeks had vanished. Climbing out of the massive four-poster bed draped in pale blue silk, she discovered hot washing water in a silver basin and a gorgeous sapphire-blue gown with gauze overlay draped over a nearby chair. After dressing quickly, she exited the room—again the doors opened in front of her as she approached—and found herself heading down the stairs and out into the back garden as if she knew where she was going. The sunlight—if that was what it could be called—was still blue, but a lighter shade than yesterday. It gave everything a cool cast, although the faceted stones and crystal seemed to glow with even more inner radiance.

Entering the intimate rose garden, she saw Asnyr standing by a fully laden breakfast table set for two. Amy frowned slightly and glanced around. "Where are the others?"

"They are still resting and recuperating, my lady. Those of royal blood heal more quickly."

Amy found herself still unable to completely relax in his presence. There was just something about his innate reserve that she didn't like. He'd have been a rake for sure in her world, and everyone knew what that meant.

He drew out her chair and she allowed herself to be seated and served tea. First things first, and all that. Nibbling on an almond pastry, she asked, "Where are all the servants?"

"Servants? Ah, well… Caoswythe Palace is a hunting lodge, you see, not one of the main residences of the royal family, so it is kept on a, shall we say, automatic setting."

Amy's eyes widened slightly at the thought that this wasn't even considered a big palace. What must the others be like?

"Princess Amy, if I may call you that?" He must have taken her dazed look as assent, because he continued: "Princess Amy, if these were normal times I would take the entire spring to scatter a different jewel every day at your feet. I would read you poetry and construct magical illusions to delight your eyes until you could see none other than me. But these are not normal times. The Elven Empire is on constant guard against intrusion from the dark forces, and the universe at large is on its knees. You are the one hope for restoring the balance and allowing my people to move freely once again through the cosmos. I would be honored if you would allow me to help you… as your husband." There should have been a question mark there, but there wasn't—it hung in the air, implied slightly but somehow beneath the dignity of the elven prince.

Amy gulped her tea. Her first proposal! This wasn't at all how she'd imagined it all that time ago giggling with her school chums in her bedchamber after lights out. She blinked and set down her cup. She had really hoped to enjoy this, but now she just felt a little out of sorts. He wasn't Ten and it should be Ten saying these beautiful things to her. Why hadn't he, anyway?

For all his reserve, Asnyr wasn't stupid or without magical powers. He sighed slightly and said, "Ah well, I didn't mean to upset you. I can see that your heart is otherwise engaged, so I'll leave you to your breakfast in peace. You should know that before you can leave this world, you and your friends must undergo truth testing. If we were bonded I could share it with you and perhaps lessen some of the shock, but that clearly is not to be. Again, my apologies." Asnyr bowed slightly from the waist and left the garden.

Amy narrowed her eyes as she poured another cup of tea from the elaborate silver pot. She didn't like to see anyone really heart sore, but it would have been slightly more flattering if he'd appeared just a tad upset. By the time she'd eaten her fill and re-entered the house, the others had emerged from their rooms and were gathered in the main hall, where yet another dining table had appeared with a full repast. Amy was a little miffed to see that no one appeared to have missed her or was even looking up at her entrance. She cleared her throat with a warning note.

Lord Kalil looked up and then sprang into action, dragging another chair to the table and seating her in it. "Ah, there you are, my dear. We thought you were still asleep." Her feathers de-ruffled slightly at that. "We were just discussing where we go from here and how to get there exactly."

"Asnyr said something about truth testing, what is that?"

Ten's eyes narrowed slightly at that. "Probably nothing to be concerned about." But he didn't sound completely convinced.

A slight shimmer in the air had everyone looking up and toward the door. The captain of the archers stood in the doorway, still dressed in the silver and black of the day before. The glowing blue beads were still braided into his long blond hair and were a striking contrast with all that black. It should have looked effeminate, but it didn't. "Prince Asnyr regrets, but his father, King Kastulf, has called him back to the capital. He has offered us, his personal guard, at your service to assist with your quest."

Everyone looked surprised when Master An was the first to speak. "Do you feel this is your personal destiny? We need no sacrifices for the sake of honor alone."

Gantnor, the captain, almost smiled but caught himself in time. "We are honored to serve the future empress."

It was the first time this was said in the open. Amy gulped a little. St. Abyn, in his usual style, whispered to her, "Don't worry, we'll probably all get killed long before that happens!" He winked at her as he said it, and she found that, curiously, that thought did make things better.

Gantnor continued without pause. "There is an elven passage to Space Station Omega just down the road. It is magic, not mechanics, so each of you must pass through the Glade of Souls first. There you will be truth tested and you may find yourself with new powers afterwards. If the risk is not to your liking, we can return you to the world whence you came, but the danger there is much higher."

Ten and St. Abyn immediately put their heads together and began whispering. Ten looked up and around the group. "Continuing via the space station may be our only viable path. There is a portal there direct to New York City where we will find the last gate. To go any other way will mean months of additional travel, and I don't think we have the time." He looked a little grim at this, but resigned. Amy wondered what he was keeping to himself. She looked around the rest of the group; they all looked open to this new experience but she wondered what "new powers" might entail.

She nodded to Gantnor. "We will proceed with your

recommendation, captain." Even Ten looked somewhat taken aback at the regal tone of her proclamation. She felt herself blushing slightly but shook it off. If she was going to be empress of the known universe, she might as well start practicing.

Gantnor gestured toward the courtyard and the group rose and followed him out. There they found the company of archers assembled in marching order, as well as fresh packs for themselves. Amy's was a quarter of the size of the men's, but when she reached down to pick it up she realized that her clothing had magically changed once again—this time to unfamiliar garb of black slacks with lots of pockets and a slick black top and jacket with even more pockets. Her hair had also braided itself into one long tail. She rather liked the new look. It seemed very practical with all those pockets.

16

On to the Space Station

Still without horses, they headed out, walking toward the horizon, and within minutes found themselves in an alpine glade. Evergreens made of thin needles of green tourmaline clustered around a misty lake. Faces seemed to appear and disappear in the mist. Gantnor paused the group on the edge, saying, "This is the Glade of Souls. For the Leanadhe it is a place to commune with our ancestors. For you, it will be something else. It will seem that everyone has disappeared until you get to the other side. So just keep walking—no matter what happens, keep walking in a straight line."

With that, the group moved forward, the humans with some trepidation after that introduction. Sure enough, each person soon found himself alone in the surreal landscape. It was as though the rest of the group had never been there.

Master An proceeded with his usual equanimity. It seemed his soul didn't have much to say either, as he emerged on the other side fairly quickly and with no visible signs of a stressful, life-changing experience. Gantnor looked nonplussed.

St. Abyn stepped forward and was surrounded by a light lavender mist. He kept walking as invisible fingers tugged at him gently from all sides. Voices of past managers hammered at him in godlike tones, deep and echoing. He saw his mother walking in front of him on the path, but she didn't look back. He ran to catch up to her, but she disappeared just as he reached to touch her shoulder. One more step and he was clear, standing next to Master An. If he had gained any new powers, he was unable to detect them, but he was glad to be done. He sank down on his heels, and for the first time really questioned his future in corporate crime.

Lord Kalil followed closely behind him on the path. He was swamped with images of a lovely pale green maiden draped in rose draperies as she rolled out pastries. She looked up from her work and smiled directly at him, adorable dimples appearing on either side of her mouth. He knew with absolutely no doubt that this would be his future bride if only he could discover what world she was on. His heart lifted with new purpose.

Amy walked down the path next and discovered that she could still see everyone. She was so bemused by that that she failed to notice that silver arabesques and traceries had appeared on her arms as she went. It was only when she reached the point where the others had stopped and St. Abyn gasped that she looked down and saw the glowing lines in her skin. She tried to pick them out but they were literally in her skin. Good thing they were pretty. Gantnor was as beside himself as an elf can get that nobody seemed to be having quite the harrowing experience he'd expected.

Ten was the last in line and he looked grimmer than ever when he caught up to the others. Amy opened her mouth to ask why, but he just shook his head and kept walking. He only stopped when he noticed her arms. Unceremoniously, he reached down and grabbed her arm, tracing the new pattern with his finger. He looked at her finally to say, "Do you know what this is?"

"Nooo…"

"These are the runes of the Imperial House. You are now publicly marked as an heir to the empty throne. Pull down your sleeves and keep them there." With that, he moved to the head of the group and began a whispered conference with Gantnor. Twenty minutes later, they arrived at what appeared to be a small blue cave.

Gantnor stopped the group. "This is the elven passage to the space station. On the other side is the power substation broom closet. Keep moving through until you reach the hallway so that we don't attract too much attention." He rolled his eyes a little at this part. If you've ever seen Space Station Omega then you'd know there's no such thing as standing out.

Walking through the elven door was like going through an automatic car wash that used silver glitter instead of water. They popped out the other side into the promised broom closet, which opened to a corridor of vending machines, each with increasingly hypnotic lights in an attempt to take out the competition. As they entered the corridor, the glitter evaporated with little golden pops, leaving them all as they had been, just a little brighter, like a brass candlestick after a good polish. Ten seemed to know where they were, as he purposefully headed off in one direction without even looking to see if anyone was following. The elven guard, picking up on the fact that a phalanx of pointy-eared blondes dressed in black might attract unwanted attention, stopped mid-corridor to glamour each other. What emerged was a ragtag crowd of disparate creatures. Amy just shook her head with astonishment at the results and kept walking.

The space station was old, built back in the days when space living seemed glamorous and people were willing to put up with small, windowless spaces because they were living a dream. Things had changed. The truly public areas like service corridors and broom closets were still institutional beige. Everything else was as bright and colorful as its owner could make it, and since those owners came from different species with different types of eyesight, things could get a little visually wild when all that creativity came together.

Ten and St. Abyn didn't seem distracted by the discordant design schemes, but Amy and Lord Kalil were getting whiplash from trying to take it all in while walking at the same time. Master An was his usual even-tempered self, but if you looked closely he frequently shook his head in dismay as he studied his feng shui compass and softly lamented the results. Amy knew him well enough at this point to guess that he was dying to stop for some evangelical conversation, but sometimes you just had to let the bad chi flow.

Amy knew they'd arrived at Ten's intended destination when he ducked inside a dark, decrepit storefront. One of the lowest dives of the entire 175-level space station, it was a font of information for those brave enough to enter. A few weeks ago, Amy would have died before entering such an establishment, but now she was past caring about respectability. She went in close on Ten's heels but felt free to look around, since he clearly didn't need her help. That she didn't even blink to see the assortment of tentacles, eye stalks, and multi-limbed beings said a lot about just how far she'd come since she'd left fat Uncle Greg. Just because she wasn't shocked didn't mean the bar residents weren't to see a woman without any makeup or strategically placed holes in her clothing. She felt the hot, sweaty feel of eyeballs between her shoulder blades just as Ten reached a long arm back and pulled her up against his side. She tried hard not to read anything into the fact that he didn't let go at that point.

There are times when the great mysteries of life (and novels) are solved unceremoniously, without a great deal of lead-up and suspense and leave the beneficiaries somewhat confused by this lack of protocol. This was one of those times. The bartender looked up when the glamour-clad elven guard came in. Even down-on-their-luck, dead-end-job bartenders tend to sit up and take notice when a crowd of forty-five randomly assorted aliens arrives at once. Cynical and tired, his eyes lit up at the sight of St. Abyn and Lord Kalil, eye catching in their individual black and white attire. But it wasn't their striking fashion sense that brought the cry, "Achmed! It's been donkey's years. Where have you been?"

Something must have clicked, because he quickly followed that with, "Wait a minute, you must be Achmed's boys! I haven't seen you since you were two months old when your parents split. You look just like your father." He sat back on his heels with satisfaction, his ginger mustache quivering with excitement.

Amy's sidekicks weren't quite so enthusiastic. They looked at each other and back at Tom, the bartender. Kalil spoke slowly: "My father was Achmed, but so are half the fathers in Araby. My mother died when I was born." He sounded a bit dismissive.

St. Abyn was equally unimpressed. "I never had a father. My mother said he was killed in the Urban Wars that followed the assassination of the Imperial Family."

"Was her name Imogen?"

"Yesssss."

"Then you are the identical twins I am talking about. Not my fault if your parents dragged you into their messy divorce and didn't tell you the truth." He seemed a bit miffed.

Ten nodded as if this all made sense. "Explains the DNA signatures."

Without saying a word, the newly reunited brothers shrugged simultaneously as if in agreement to table it for later. Amy smiled happily. She liked happy endings, and two brothers finding each other across the cosmos? It was nice.

The group said goodbye to the elven guard, who promised to stay on the space station for a bit to see if there was any noise of the Originists. Gantnor pressed a small silver whistle into Amy's hands. "If you need further assistance—on any world or time—give that three blasts. Someone will come to you." He bowed low, and the glamoured elves faded into the eclectic crowd.

The rest of them took the lift down to sublevel -35. It was a tight fit because Lord Kalil and St. Abyn insisted on bringing along the big stuffed pink unicorns they'd won on the carnival strip on sublevel -5. They said they had to rebuild their childhood memories as brothers. Ten had rolled his eyes but allowed it, as he said it would make good camouflage where they were going. He'd had his own minute of relaxation. Amy had caught him staring in a shop window that appeared to sell exotic hand-combat weapons like nothing ever seen on Earth. She'd made a mental note for his birthday, but right now she just wanted everyone to get a move on. This NYC sounded as close as she would get to seeing Ten's home, and she was desperate to try and figure him out. He didn't write poetry to her eyelids as far as she knew, and he certainly didn't treat her as an Incomparable, but she rather liked him anyway.

When the door pinged open at sublevel -35, they could see

nothing but beige-painted corridors as far as the eye could see. The lighting was dim, as though even the corridors didn't really expect any visitors. St. Abyn shoved his unicorn at his brother and took out his little compass-like thing, simultaneously moving to the head of the group while looking down at it. He led the way, except that at every intersection Ten would pull him back and peer around the corner before motioning everyone forward. After about the fifteenth intersection, they walked down a hallway that was suspiciously similar to the one where they'd started. Except that St. Abyn paused abruptly in the middle in front of an equally beige door in the middle of the beige wall. It had no markings of any kind, but Ten seemed confident as he reached for his little penlight with one hand and for the latch with his other.

Amy held her breath in anticipation. And let it out again with a rush of disappointment when the space beyond the door revealed itself to be another broom closet. It was not lost on her that she recognized all the implements in it, from mop to bucket to dusters. Apparently some things were the same across the continuum. Nobody else seemed too concerned, however, as Ten and St. Abyn began clearing off the shelves, tossing the contents in the corner, and then quickly moving the shelving.

"We can't cover our tracks," Ten said as an aside.

St. Abyn looked concerned for a minute and then moved a broken chair under the interior doorknob. "That should keep for a bit."

Lord Kalil was stuck holding the stuffed unicorns and beginning to look a little less sure about that. Master An was gently waving his staff in soft, circular motions, giving off a lavender light as he did so.

When the shelving was cleared away, a portal was revealed, not dissimilar to the others except this one was Art Deco, triangles and dots marched around the perimeter, and the control panel had a snazzy geometric design. "Everyone ready?" Ten inquired with his finger poised over the middle button. Everyone nodded and then the light behind the door began to swirl orange. They filed through and into a dim concrete passage. Amy wasn't at all sure that they had really gone anywhere, but the rest seemed pretty confident. There was a stale, mucky smell emanating from the space.

17

The Wonders of New York City

Lord Kalil was the first to ask, "Where exactly are we?"

"We're in the service passage beneath the Holland Tunnel."

Kalil looked oddly excited. "If I hadn't been born a sheik, I would have been a civil engineer. Think of the tunnels I could have built beneath the sand…"

After climbing stairs for what seemed forever, they emerged out in the open behind some sad-looking bushes. Without looking back, Ten headed off at a determined pace and the rest, now used to this, fell in behind. Fifteen minutes later, he was leading them down steps and into the subway. At this point Amy's eyes were getting tired from being so wide open. Ten leaned down to whisper in her ear: "If you're going to be empress of the known universe, you can certainly handle the Big Apple." Amy looked around frantically for a giant fruit but saw only the pink unicorns, now looking a little dingy in Kalil's arms. She gritted her teeth and stood up straight. As annoyed as she was, he was right—she'd better practice her royal demeanor. She decided to see if she could look down her nose at Ten, a challenge only because he was at least eight inches taller. She stopped when she felt herself going cross-eyed. When the subway doors blew open, Ten pushed them all out on the platform and counted noses like a kindergarten teacher. Satisfied, he gestured up the stairs.

A few minutes later, Amy found herself in Central Park. It was the closest she had felt to home since all this began. The blue sky shone down over clumps of daffodils along the path, and the sun had a welcome warmth. That was until the rollerbladers came at her like charging Ichnitanids. Except those horrible things had just tried to kill her; these seemed intent on flattening her in the process. She moved behind Ten, who just strode forward through the crowd like nothing was the matter.

Because she was still using Ten's broad back as a shield against the oncoming hordes of people, she missed seeing the cool blond woman sitting on the park bench. But that certainly didn't stop the woman from spotting Ten.

"Tenneson! What a surprise!"

Amy felt the silent groan emanate from him just before she saw the air kisses come over his shoulders. "Caroline." It was neither question nor invitation, but the woman didn't seem in the least concerned.

Amy coughed quietly. Ten turned and looked at her as though he'd forgotten her very existence, and then performed cursory introductions. "Monsieur St. Abyn, Lord Kalil, Master An, Amy, this is Caroline—we used to work together."

"Oh, we did much more than that! Why, remember that time in Baghdad when you were prepared to protect my body with yours, all night long if necessary?" She raised one eyebrow and smiled a cool, intimate smile while grabbing one arm as if to lead him away.

Amy decided there was no time like the present to practice being royal. She grabbed Ten's other arm. "Excuse us, Caroline,

but we have important business. Some other time, perhaps?"
She didn't wait for a reply and put all her force of will into the
hand on his bicep.

Master An leaned forward slightly to adjust her sleeve, which
had slipped to show a hint of the silver tracery on her arm.

"Really, Tenneson? She's a little Bohemian for you, don't you
think? Or perhaps there's something else going on."

Her light blue eyes narrowed suspiciously beneath carefully
tinted brows as she surveyed the ragtag little group. "Headed
toward the museum, were you? Mind if I tag along?"

"Yes," Ten ground out through his clenched teeth. Caroline
only looked more amused.

With his left hand, Ten plucked Amy's off his right arm, but
held her hand in a bone-crushing grasp as he tugged her down
a side path away from their original direction. The rest hurried
to keep up. Amy glanced over her shoulder to see the other
woman stretch languidly then begin to follow in at a saunter.
"She's following us!"

"I know," Ten gritted out.

"I have a lot of questions for you!"

"I'm sure." He sounded a little more his old sardonic self.

He kept the group moving at a stiff pace for a few more
blocks before ducking into an alley behind a row of shops. One
grimy, gray metal door stood open with steam billowing out.
Ten gestured them all inside just as Caroline stuck her head
around the street corner. Amy made no attempt to hide her
expression of astonishment. She was beginning to wonder if
she knew him at all. Last in the door, Ten shut it and threw the
bolt before looking around with a world-weary eye. Just then,
a booming voice came from the next room: "What fucking
fool shut the door?" The voice was quickly followed by a giant

bald man with muscles bigger than Ten's. "Ten!" He looked and sounded as delighted as a seven-year-old on Christmas morning. Manly hugs followed, which Ten suffered without losing his composure. "I never thought I'd see you again after you went north. Are you rejoining us in the human race or staying with the bears?"

"Sully, my friends and I need a quiet place to talk and then to make use of your private entrance."

"Sure, sure. Use the front room we don't open for another three hours. The entrance is where you left you it. Hey, do you still have that mangy cat you named after Sergeant F'ing Asshole?"

"If you mean Wallace, then yes, he's still alive. He's fine."

"You have a cat?" This time it was Amy's eyebrow that went up with sardonic amusement.

"I don't have him. He's just old and a little down on his luck. He comes by for a meal every now and then."

"So yes, you have a cat is what you're saying. Where is he now?"

"He's staying with a friend."

"Are you going to go back and get him?"

"What's with all the questions about a damn cat? I told you I don't expect to go back to anything."

"Hmmph. I'm looking forward to making Wallace's acquaintance." She smirked.

Sully continued gathering plates and glasses onto a tray. "You guys hungry? Today's special is dumplings. On the house!"

Lord Kalil's eyes lit with delight, which was quickly spotted by the business-savvy restaurateur, who began filling plates. With that, he led them into the front room, which turned out to be the dining room of a small restaurant fronting the street. They sat down at a round table in the corner just as Caroline walked past outside, glancing in as she did so. St. Abyn opened his mouth to speak, but Ten spoke first with distinct amusement. "Don't worry—Sully hates her guts. He won't let her in here, and as long as we don't shout she can't hear what we say."

Lord Kalil just looked his question while stuffing his mouth with a dumpling. When he could talk again, he asked, "Why does he hate her? She seems very accommodating."

"She is that. She accommodated herself to some of the national art treasures we were supposed to be guarding. She's an international art negotiator: buys, sells, and trades for hostaged works deemed treasures of humanity. If a few of the minor pieces that aren't so grand go home in a diplomatic pouch, well, she's okay with that. Sully isn't."

"What is she to you? Did you court her?" Amy spoke low and softly but intently.

Ten looked momentarily taken aback at the word "court," but then he sighed heavily and chose his words very carefully: "Nothing, Amy. We passed some time together a long time ago. I never courted her and certainly have no intention of doing so."

Amy wasn't quite as wet behind the ears as she had been, so her eyes narrowed slightly at this but she let it drop. "Why did we come here instead of continuing to the museum?"

"Because Caroline is nosy and we don't need an audience for this. Last I heard, she works at the museum." He paused and then continued slowly, "I'm not absolutely sure, but I think she may have some transport privileges. She knows more than she should for an average citizen of 21st-century New York." He paused at that. "I've seen objects with her that came from other worlds"—he nodded at Amy—"things like your necklace, although nothing with such power. She could have picked them up along the way in this world, but…"

St. Abyn nodded thoughtfully. "It's always easier to fence things between worlds, but it does take some talent to find just enough overlap that the items don't stand out too much. It's amazing the prices 'original finish' can fetch in the antiques market. If a few things move forward a bit in time without lingering in the intervening centuries, well, who is harmed?"

They made their plans sitting at Sully's table with the red checked cloth while eating dumplings. City dust danced in the sunshine that streamed in through the windows. Amy counted three times that Caroline walked by outside. It seemed that Sully's restaurant had a basement storage room with a door that led to an old service tunnel that just happened to link up to one beneath the museum. They would wait below the city streets for nightfall when the museum was closed and then make their way to the portal to the Lost City. Nervous now that the big moment was upon her, Amy started picking at the wax on the wine bottle candle in the middle of the table. "Tenneson. What kind of a name is that? And why don't you use it?"

"Because I don't like it. Which Caroline knows full well."

Amy wasn't sure what to do with that. So she sighed and stuffed her hands in some of her many pockets and slouched in her chair. She wanted to get this whole Lost City thing over with so she could figure out her relationship with him. But he probably just thought of her as a silly girl and would be on his way as soon as possible. Then she remembered that shared horse ride and perked up. Maybe not…

18

The Big Reveal

Later that night, they made their way through New York's subterranean passages. Rats made everyone except Ten squeak a bit; even Master An lost some of his calm when presented with that much damp yin energy. Ten still insisted on checking each intersection, even though none of them could imagine what besides the rats could possibly be waiting to ambush them down there. Finally they emerged in the lower levels of the museum, where racks upon racks of industrial metal shelving held all the objects too interesting to put on display. His eyes forward, Ten laid down the law to the man behind him: "St. Abyn, don't touch!" St. Abyn put his hands back in his pockets and pouted slightly.

Prosaically they took an elevator up to the main level. The museum was eerily quiet. Long shadows fell against the cases from the security lights. As they made their way toward the section of the Ancients, their footsteps echoed unnaturally loudly in the empty space where a thousand feet could run undetected during the day. Amy's stomach felt like it was in her throat. She wasn't sure why. A month ago she hadn't known about any of this, but now people wanted to kill her and her new friends and she desperately did not want them to succeed.

"There it is." Ten's voice, soft and unemotional, alerted the group. Amy jerked to attention as the group gathered in front of the far wall. The entire surface was covered with blindingly white marble panels. Each one was intricately carved with flowers and rabbit figures. There was a shallow threshold like a doorstep in front of the two biggest panels that reached floor to ceiling. To the right was a small label that described it as a decorative pediment and frieze in the Phoenician style, date and origin unknown.

"But how?" Amy said, bewildered.

Ten responded while the others gathered their wits. "It was moved here intact twenty-five years ago, once the intergalactic courts decreed that there were no standing heirs to the royal family. It's a portal, not a real door, so it should remain functional as long as the electronics remain within the frame."

"Wouldn't the Originists have just removed them?"

"They might, but not much point. There are several portals that lead there; this just happens to be the most direct, official one, and it's also not that hard for someone that knows what they're doing to reprogram any portal to that destination. It's just that it's illegal, would take a couple of weeks, be impossible to test or operate without a royal, and, well, this is easier."

"Oh, okay. Well, what do I do?" She hated that her voice wasn't as steady as a good heroine's should be.

Ten took the pendant out of his pocket and, holding it lightly in his hand, walked toward the portal. Standing directly in front of the door, he raised the pendant so that it was level with a circular design in the carving. As he stood there unmoving, lights began to appear within the stone, glowing oddly blue, green, and gold from behind the white marble. The structure began to hum softly, like it was waking up from a long sleep. Ten softly stepped forward and put his hand flat against the central panel. It didn't budge. He pressed again and then stepped back, handing the pendant to Amy. As he stepped back, some of the lights dimmed but the humming continued. "Just do what I did," he instructed, "but when you press the panel, if you feel any movement, stop until we're all standing with you. If you go without us, this time we won't be able to follow." Amy nodded jerkily and took the pendant from his warm hand. Hers felt cold and icy as she walked forward, holding the pendant up as he had done.

The lights flickered back on until the entire structure was blazing. As she walked up to the central panels, she could feel the vibration in all her bones; it was like her body was humming along with it. Gently placing her left hand that was holding the pendant against the panel, she felt warmth and an odd sense of welcome emanating from the stone. She pressed gently and felt her hand move through the stone. It was such a shocking sensation that she jerked it back and ran to the others. But they were jubilant. Ten, grinning, kissed her without a thought for the others and tossed her into the air before hugging her tightly. The others barely noticed this unusual display of emotion, as they were dancing with excitement. Maybe they hadn't seen her hand go in to the door? No, it turned out they had but didn't think anything of it. It was a high-security portal, after all, not the sort you risked leaving open.

"So, how do we all go, then?" she asked, exasperated at always being the one caught off guard.

"We'll hold hands," St. Abyn said. "Like a human chain. It should allow us all through if we retain some kind of direct link with you."

"All right?" Ten kissed her again—for what seemed to go on

for eons, not that she was complaining. Her eyes widened; this must be really going to his head. She knew the others were trying to match make by putting them together as often as possible but it hadn't seemed to have much effect. She'd seen St. Abyn pull his brother back in the tunnels just an hour ago so that she'd be walking directly behind Ten instead of farther back. But Ten seemed oblivious to their efforts and appeared to take every care not to imply any attachment to anyone observing. Fully distracted by the mysteries of the male psyche, she forgot to be scared and, taking his hand in her left one, walked steadily forward with the pendant raised once again in her right hand. The others quickly linked up behind Ten, the chain ending with Master An. As the lights began blazing again at full force, Amy pushed her hand into the door and then stepped forward. It felt a little like walking through molasses. As she was almost completely through, shouting came from the far end of the gallery. "Quickly!" Ten said in her ear. She pushed forward completely and kept walking as the molasses sensation suddenly gave way to a paved courtyard under a star-studded sky. Ten kept a grasp on her hand as she instinctively went to let go and pushed her gently forward to make room for the others.

Master An soon emerged, his lavender robes glowing in the starlight and whipping about him with the unexpected speed of his movements. "Oh my," he exclaimed. "That was close. They almost touched my arm."

"Well, not much they can do about it now," said St. Abyn with satisfaction, "unless they've got a spare registered royal or one with a pendant tucked away somewhere."

"We aren't going to stay here forever, are we?" asked Amy. "I can't even see what this place is, but if we're the only ones on the entire planet it's going to be hard to go shopping."

"No—we need to restore the balance but we won't stay here forever. Let's set up camp and get some sleep. There will be a lot to see tomorrow." The group signaled agreement by simply reaching for the packs and going through the tasks that were now routine to lay out bedrolls and settle for the night. They left off the fire, not having the light to see any obvious fuel. Ten took the first watch, sitting comfortably on his bedroll, next to Amy's as she and the others lay down. Amy wished she had a guidebook for this world now that they had finally arrived. In truth, she hadn't really believed it would happen. It's very difficult to be the reigning empress of a planet you haven't even seen.

19

Exploring the Lost City

Bright sunlight danced on Amy's eyelids. She sat up, eager to see where they'd landed after all the hard work to get there. This, then, was the Lost City. Quite frankly, Amy thought it needed a good dusting. Then maybe, just maybe, it might begin to resemble the majestic Greek temples she had so admired in the engravings featured in the Ladies' Scientific Review. Huge columns lay askew on the jungle floor, vines coming up and over, obscuring whole buildings. The light was dim, as though someone had left the whole place on a vacation setting. The humid heat was penetrating, so Amy unconsciously pushed her sleeves up. The landscape brightened immediately. The others gasped and whirled around as though looking for an enemy to blame for the clear yellow sun now visible in the sky. They continued gaping when they saw Amy's arms. For what had been silver tracery was now blazing gold, emitting a strange light of its own. And the lines had spread down the backs of her hands up her arms and across her back, although nobody would notice that last part for some time.

They continued looking around, the younger men showing off a bit by clambering up the vines. Amy and Master An stuck to the cleared paths that looked as though the vines had known better than to grow across. They weren't cut. The vines had grown back onto themselves as if hitting an invisible wall. A shout came from one of the brothers off to the left and the others hurried in that direction.

When they arrived in the small clearing between huge trees, it was to find a small collapsed marble building covered in vines. "In here," exclaimed the excited voice, and with that clue they finally could see the narrow passage through the exposed doorway. After climbing through, they discovered that Amy's arms now lit the dark space and nobody had to hold a flashlight. Lord Kalil was dancing slightly in place with excitement. In his hands was a glowing blue orb about eight inches in diameter. When he suddenly dropped his hands, the others gasped and reached theirs out. But the orb didn't fall; it hung in midair, making an odd humming noise. Then it suddenly took off, dipping slightly to exit the room and then picking up speed through the trees.

Amy looked around the small room and smiled. A charming frieze of rabbits decorated the crumbling walls—they were in various stages of an activity involving a small blue ball, just like the one that had just flown off. She looked back at Ten, only to find him frozen in place, his face considerably paler; brackets framed his mouth. He visibly shook it off and began moving things about quickly. Declaring the space clear, he motioned everyone to exit the way they'd come in. Lord Kalil looked mournfully in the direction the blue ball had gone before following the others back to the main path. A little farther on, they entered what appeared to be a main town square. It too was vineless but dusty. A long, colonnaded building fronted one side, and Amy wandered into one of the nearby doorways. The place was filled with books, all still neatly on their shelves,

but the spines were labeled in a language she had never seen
before. She picked a book at random and opened it, hoping to
see what it was about from the contents. It was full of diagrams
and formulas. She passed it to St. Abyn, who had come in
behind her, and he whistled quietly.

"Ten."

"Yeah?" came from a distance.

"You might want to see this."

"Coming."

Ten came in and took the book, flipping through the pages.
"Dammit. This would have come in handy a few years back."

"What is it?" Amy inquired, really, really tired of being left
out of all this information everyone else seemed to have.

"It's an instruction manual for building a new portal to
a world that doesn't have one. See, here are the electrical
pathways and the diagram for forming the connections to the
ion stream."

"This place alone could change the balance of the universe."

Amy felt a little uneasy at that. And for some reason an image
of the cool blond Caroline came to her mind. Surely as empress
she would get a palace guard and staff? She didn't think she
could manage being empress and librarian at the same time.

They all liked a good book, but eventually decided it was
time to move on. They left Master An there, as he complained
he was feeling the heat and wouldn't be much use for the heavy
stuff anyway. He settled into a deep window seat with a stack
of books and began turning pages happily in the dusty gloom.

They walked across to the adjacent side of the square, where
a series of smaller buildings were arranged, each with a façade
featuring a different geometric shape: circle, square, triangle,
and so on. There were five in all. Amy instinctively headed into

the middle one with a rectangle and found a simple stone room with built-in benches on all sides. On a far wall was a giant sheet of beaten silver—or at least it looked like silver until she walked closer and the entire sheet came alive. It was as though she was on the upper balcony looking down on the Bath Assemblies as the dancers whirled. Why, there was her friend Clarisse! Dancing with her brother Freddy's commanding officer, gazing adoringly into his eyes. Amy peered closer. Her last letter from Clarisse had sworn that she hated the fellow—this view sure showed a different picture. Tearing her gaze away from trying to find familiar faces in the crowd, she noticed several small dials arranged vertically to the left of the image. She began twisting them just to see what would happen. A wildly different view appeared; this one was a forest scene where all the trees were orange. Red hairy people—well, they kind of looked like people, but it was a stretch—were seated around a campfire. They seemed to be singing, or trying to. That's the difficulty with alien civilizations. It's always hard to tell what is just simply different taste versus complete lack of talent. It certainly didn't sound like anything Amy wanted to hear more of, so she swiftly turned the dial all the way to the right and the screen turned off.

She randomly pressed some buttons near the dials, and in the middle of the room a doorway rose up out of the floor; it was just the jamb without a door, but the center was murky, swirling crystal. St. Abyn almost walked into it, but a last-minute shout from his brother just behind him saved him from joining the Astyrx on Cestus V for an impromptu holiday. Amy quickly turned all the dials back completely to the left. Finally. Something interesting she had found and could use without relying on the others for information. Maybe she'd even get to explain it to them.

"That blue sphere is back, and it brought friends," St. Abyn announced once he'd recovered his breath.

20

The Mystery is Solved

Sure enough, out on the plaza area was a gang of blue spheres in different sizes, roughly six to twelve inches in diameter. Suspended at different elevations, they bounced and swayed slightly with the breeze. When Amy walked down the steps of the building, they moved into a central vibrating mass and then dispersed rapidly away into the surrounding countryside. Amy looked around for someone that was prepared to explain this. There was a unanimity of shrugs. "Perhaps we should do something of a perimeter check," Ten suggested grimly. "The mysteries are appearing faster than the old ones are getting solved." Leaving Master An behind to try and come up with something innovative for supper, the rest headed out.

A fine mist arose quickly, separating Ten and Amy from the others. It shrouded the trees until they had no outline and were barely discernible. Amy called out to the others with concern, but there was no response. Ten seemed on edge, so Amy stayed close to him. The mist was even thicker now, except for one path that led away from the direction they had come. There it seemed to promise clearing skies, and the path was obvious and unobstructed. Ten shrugged, and they headed down the path. She looked behind to see that the fog was filling in behind them but never seemed to catch up. The path ahead stayed clear as day.

"Are we being led somewhere?"

"Looks like it."

"Should we really be doing this?"

"Something with more power than we have wants to talk to us. I figure we might as well get it over with and maybe learn something."

The path continued around the outskirts of the ruins they had yet to explore. Beyond that were some dark, gothic woods, and then a small, intact building with a central dome and ionic columns in the front. The windows were glowing blue as they approached. The door was opened by a woman dressed in a long green pleated gown with gold cords. Her dark hair was bound up with a silver chain and she was holding a clipboard. "Welcome, Ten and Amy. Do come in. I was expecting you."

Amy was feeling brave, in large part because this strange woman resembled her teachers from Miss Marchant's Academy, at least in demeanor. None of them had been allowed to wear anything besides navy serge. "Who are you? I was told this entire planet was desolate."

"Oh, it is. Absolutely right, my dear." The woman smiled kindly. "I'm not a person as you would define it more an embodiment of this place—just call me ma'am."

Ten sighed. "One of the Elementals, aren't you?"

"Why, yes! Seems like nobody remembers we exist anymore." She looked a little downcast but then perked up and looked back at her clipboard. "Let's see—you two are signed up for individual truth testing. I'm so excited to finally get this phase going. Follow me." And with that chipper note, she turned around and headed back inside.

Amy wasn't so sure. "Wait a minute! What truth testing? I haven't signed up for anything. How could I in this place?"

The woman turned back. "Oh, you were signed up the moment of your birth. I mean, it did take quite a bit of effort to get your mother out of this place. We didn't do that just for the fun of it."

Amy wasn't sure whether she was using the royal "we." She tried to peer into the interior to see if there were other people lurking about.

Ten whispered in her ear, "Elementals are the spirits that pre-date people. Think of them like the Greek gods. She's the guardian of this place."

"And this truth testing?" she whispered back.

"It's the only path forward, but likely to be... unpleasant."

"What's my other choice?"

"Turning around and going back home while the universe descends into anarchy."

"Oh. Well, in that case, let's get on with it."

With that, she headed through the door after the strange woman walking down a central corridor to the back room. There in the space under the dome was a room fitted out with all kinds of electronics around the perimeter. Screens and monitors filled the wall space, while the dome itself was a swirling vortex of light that seemed to have no end. On the floor were two round raised daises.

The woman gestured to each of them. "Up you go. Ten, you're over there. Amy, here." Amy watched Ten mount the steps like a tired old man before bracing himself in the center. She wondered what he was expecting to happen. He didn't look at her, so she turned and walked up the steps to the other platform. Without further ado, a column of goo descended straight out of the vortex above down to the floor. Where it brushed her clothes and skin it just felt like warm soup, but when she tried to push her hand out, the substance resisted. Strangely, she didn't have any problems breathing or opening her eyes, but she couldn't see past the goo, which was an emerald green in color.

"Welcome, Amy!" a kindly, avuncular voice said in her head. "We're delighted you're finally here. Let's see—this shouldn't take too long, because we already have most of your vitals on file. We've been watching you very closely, you know. Very closely!"

"Why am I here, then?" She noticed this was said in her head; her lips seemed frozen.

"Just protocol. We have to make sure you're ready to be empress of the known universe and all that. Not much good having an unwilling empress, now, would it?"

"I suppose not."

"Hmmm, well, you don't seem particularly excited about the prospect, but generally that's a good thing. Megalomania has its own problems. Now then, I'm done with my scans—there are just a few behavior tests we need to do."

The voice kind of clicked off and Amy saw the goo change from opaque emerald to absolutely clear. She looked over at Ten and saw that he was enveloped in the same goo, but his eyes were rolled back in his head in agony. His knees were sagging and she could see the pulse in his throat pounding furiously.

"What are you doing to him? Stop it! Stop it!" she screamed as she pushed her way through the force field with sheer willpower and stumbled down the steps of the pedestal. Pushing her hand through the energy field around Ten was not nearly so difficult, more like reaching into a full bathtub. She reached through and grabbed Ten's hand. Two things happened when she did: Ten's heartbeat began to slow back down to a normal rate and the school mistress checked something off on her clipboard.

"Excellent! You passed that one with flying colors. I knew you had it in you."

Amy shook her head in disbelief and turned her attention back to Ten. His fingers slowly curled around hers. She could tell it was taking great effort, and his face made it clear he was still dealing with something else. A part of him obviously knew she was there, though, so she did her best to send strength through their clasped hands. Unbeknownst to her, she did actually have this power, but it would be years before she learned to command it at will.

The woman with the clipboard pointed to one of the screens on the wall. "You can watch here. It's pretty much what he's seeing."

Amy held on to Ten's hand but half turned to see the screen. She watched as translucent holographic rabbits the size of full-grown men maneuvered much more solid electronic equipment over and around Ten, prone on a ground tarp. Palm trees were in the distance. His face was writhing in agony and the tendons in his arms and legs were straining against the ropes that tied him to bamboo poles. The image was replaced by one of the rabbit creatures, now filling the screen but still translucent. "We are deeply sorry, young man, that we had to take such drastic measures, but our resources were limited by existing now only in holographic form." He looked bemusedly down at his see-through furry fingers, longer than a real rabbit's. "We whose image you see died millennia ago, and we could only guess at what would be needed. When the time came, we had to use what was at hand. I'm sure you now see it was worth the sacrifice." He beamed a smile directly at Amy. She jumped.

Ten's jaw was clamped tight. "What did you do to me?"

"Oh, didn't you know? Oh dear, oh dear, oh dear. I thought you knew. Didn't we make that clear?"

Ten just glared. The rabbit sighed. "All we did was alter your DNA a little." He glanced over at Amy again. "Just to ensure the continuity of the royal line. I'm sure we told you your mission was vitally important to the survival of the space-time continuum and would require the ultimate sacrifice." He paused and looked questioningly at Ten.

"Oh, you did. You bastard. You made it very clear I was going to die."

"Die! Who said anything about dying?" He seemed to catch on and then blushed. (If you've never seen a giant holographic rabbit blush, thank your lucky stars.) "Errr, umm, well, you see…" The hologram actually fidgeted. "The Oryctolan have always been more of an intellectual bent. We don't like, er, physical intimacy. It gets in the way of deep meditation. It's part of why we died out," he ended glumly.

"Are you seriously saying that you put me through hell just to put me out to stud?" Ten glanced down at Amy before glaring back at the rabbit. Amy met his gaze and then looked away, blushing.

"Well, we had to ensure that your combined genes would produce royal offspring—usually it's about twenty-five percent, but under the circumstances we couldn't afford those odds so we, umm… redid the original modifications on you too just to improve the odds." He looked a little bashful—all this talk of mating was hard on the rabbit, even the holographic one.

Amy sighed in sympathy. She wasn't too comfortable hearing about it either. "Then how come he couldn't open the portal?"

"That needed a direct descendent, which he isn't, but everything else he can now do, and your children will be able to do everything you can."

Amy was even more embarrassed. They hadn't even discussed marriage, and here their future children's talents were being openly discussed. "How did you even know we would meet?"

"What would have happened if I had died?" Ten was clearly doing his best not to lose his temper.

The rabbit tried to answer them both at once. "Well, we did some long-range statistical analysis, ran quite a few personality tests, and finally decided you were the most likely. And if you had been killed, well, we at least lessened the chances of that with your added powers. And"—he shrugged—"worst case, Amy would have had to have quite a few more children [he blushed again] or the space-time continuum would finally descend into utter chaos." He paused and looked down at a wristwatch. "I'm very sorry, but I'm out of time. This operation used up the last of the solnadium battery powering me—the others were turned off years ago." He sniffed sadly. "Goodbye." With a blink, the hologram was gone.

The goo around Ten disappeared into smoke at the same time.

He and Amy both gazed blankly at the now-empty screen. Amy was the first to recover, and she looked up at Ten sadly, sighed, and reached up on her tiptoes to kiss him on the cheek. He looked down at her quizzically.

"You don't have to, you know. Marry me and all that." When he didn't immediately reply, she looked down at the floor, scuffing the toe of her boot with embarrassment.

"Later, Amy," he said softly. "We still have an audience."

She looked up, startled, and he nodded toward the

schoolmistress.

"Well, I'm glad to see that's all sorted. Amy, you've passed your evaluation with flying colors. Please get back on the podium, there's a dear."

Amy reluctantly left Ten's side to climb back up the steps slowly and position herself in the center of the circular dais. It took all her will power not to run out of the room, but she had a strong feeling there was no running away from any of this. A column of gold and silver sparkles, with a few purple ones mixed in for effect, descended on her, forming a column of energy. It tingled a little. She looked down and gasped—the tracery on the backs of her hands and arms had rearranged itself into glowing symbols of power. Each one she understood and knew how to use. This for eliciting truth, that one for assisting with weather, another for distributing justice. She reached a hand up unconsciously to her face and her fingernail clicked against something hard in passing. She reached up and pulled down a delicate crystal crown that had appeared on her head. It too had signs of power in what looked like frost crystals, but was in fact the rare semi-sentient mineral ignatium. When she put it back on her head, it immediately arranged itself correctly, her hair as well, with the added benefit of a light scalp massage.

21

Claiming Her Birthright

Amy walked out of the small building in the woods as an empress. The crown seemed to dance on her head, and every now and then a tendril would reach down and tickle her ear. When that happened, the crown positively bounced as though it were giggling to itself. Amy looked back to make sure Ten was still there. He was, looking war weary and inscrutable, but the building was gone. The light blue sky of late afternoon had reappeared, the mist had vaporized, and all that stood where they had been was a circle of trees surrounding a small pool. A frog croaked somewhere in the bracken. She sighed to herself and turned back. She wanted to talk to Ten, really talk. She didn't think she minded the thought of making babies with him. Really, not at all. But she was furious at the thought that he might be forced into it. A lady had her pride. But she wasn't sure how to broach the topic, so she just focused on getting back to find the others.

About the tenth time the crown tickled her, Amy had had enough and stopped dead in the path. "Look you… thing. Stop it, I've had enough. One more time and I'm taking you off and sticking you in a drawer!" The crown immediately stopped bouncing, and Amy could feel it droop slightly, conforming to the shape of her head. She sighed. Now she had temperamental jewelry to deal with as well. She reached up and patted it gently. It perked up a little.

A loud overhead chime dinged (odd when you're outside on an abandoned planet), followed by a standard recorded voice— the kind heard in airports and train stations anywhere in the cosmos. "Equilibrium has been restored. Repeat: equilibrium has been restored. Standard entrance portals will open in five, four, three, two, one. Standard entrance portals are now open." Another ding of the chime.

Amy looked around for either the voice or the portals it had mentioned, but Ten wasn't so analytical. With an "Oh, shit!" he grabbed her by the upper arm and started running. The crown thing put out extra tentacles to grip her head so it wouldn't fall off. Amy was out of breath when they arrived back at the central square.

The others were shouting their names frantically. St. Abyn was the first to spot them. "There they are! Where have you guys been—did you hear? We've been looking all over for you."

Ten just nodded, breathing deeply to catch his breath. He'd half carried Amy while running full out. She didn't think her feet had touched the ground more than one stride in ten. "Get her inside now!"

St. Abyn nodded and picked up Amy and tossed her over his shoulder. He ran toward the building they were camping out in, Lord Kalil close behind him. Master An waited at the entrance, and as soon as they were past the doorjamb he began waving his staff and chanting. Swirls of smoke filled the courtyard and then Master An came inside. "I have discouraged the bad chi from entering, but it cannot be completely blocked if it insists on coming. But I have good news. I have located a dragon hill on the other side of the river. If I must, I can awaken it."

"A dragon! There's no such thing… is there?" Amy realized that bottom was now up and most of the rules of the universe she'd grown up with now only applied to one tiny corner of it.

"Of course there are! Just not many awake, is all. They tend to get overexcited and they eat a lot." With that, Master An settled down to make some tea and await further developments. Amy peered around the mostly closed door just in time to see Ten heading out beyond the far end of the square. He was keeping to the shadows but moving swiftly.

"Where is he going?" she asked the others.

"Reconnaissance. Nobody is as good as Ten. It's like he's got a seventh sense with turbo boost," St. Abyn said.

Amy thought back to what the holographic rabbit had said and wondered if that wasn't actually true. "Well, why then? Shouldn't he be here with us?"

"Not with over twenty portals now open. Each one of which could be the door the Originists use to try and finish the job."

"Twenty! But Chichen only had two."

"Chichen is a total backwater. This is the center of power throughout all time and space. It requires a lot of doors."

Lord Kalil spoke up: "Ten will close the ones down that he can reach, especially those nearby. That will at least make it take longer for the bad guys to reach us."

"How long is that, do you think?" Amy chewed on her lip. She didn't want Ten getting killed, especially not before she knew how he really felt.

"A couple of minutes to a couple of years, depending on which door and what they find there. Nobody has been on this planet in decades. There used to be all kinds of fantastical creatures, but nobody knows which were native and which were not. Everything sentient was forced to leave after the assassinations."

As it turned out, they had just a few hours. When night fell, they extinguished their campfire so as not to attract attention until Ten came back with a report. Lord Kalil offered to take the first watch, just in case. Amy curled up on her pallet and tried to take the crown off, but it clung to her head so she finally gave up and put her head on the pillow. The crown moved over and made a kind of softly glittering sleeping cap.

The building door creaked open with just a whisper of air but no sound. Lord Kalil sat up straighter, but Ten headed straight for Amy. He crouched down beside her. "Listen, Amy, they're already here. They must have been massing by several different portals just waiting for the opportunity. I saw Caroline come through with a force of about two hundred about an hour ago just to the south of the city. She must have been working with them all along. I don't like this, but I need you and your powers to see what we're up against. You ready?"

"But I don't know what to do with my powers!" The crown had reshaped itself to its most royal shape when she'd sat up as Ten approached. It gave her a soft, encouraging nudge that forced a smile. But she really didn't know how to do anything yet. She'd been hoping for some tutor to appear or something. The lady with the clipboard seemed the most likely candidate.

"I know, but I have some general ideas and I think your crown knows the rest. Mostly I just need your presence. Try to keep your head down, okay?"

She nodded and took his hand to stand up. Lord Kalil had also stood, and raised an eyebrow at Ten, who just shook his head.

He led Amy out of that building and into the next, where

they'd discovered a subterranean passage just the day before. Once the door was closed and they were past where any light could escape, he took out his penlight. Amy stared. His face was covered with green streaks. "What happened to you?"

Ten looked blank and then he grinned. The devil was in his eyes as he trailed a finger down the delicate alabaster of her cheek. "This will never do," he said cheerfully. She widened her violet eyes in shock and gazed at him mutely, not sure what to say to this man that had just changed before her eyes. He seemed to be genuinely having a good time. He reached into his pocket and took out a small jar. After removing the lid, he stuck in his index finger. When he brought it back out, it was covered with an olive-green compound. He carefully began tracing patterns across her cheeks and forehead. "You need camouflage, sweetheart," he explained as he dipped his finger in the jar again then began drawing it down the sensitive side of her neck and toward the neckline of her shirt.

Amy held herself still, afraid to even move lest she give in to the temptation to hurl him to the ground and rip his clothes off. Just when she thought she could not stand another second, he dipped his finger in he jar and began retracing the green streaks, now faded and cracked, on his own face. There was something about the decoration that gave him a wild, pagan look, even with his neatly cropped blond hair, which he'd rubbed with mud to take the shine off. When Ten finished, he stuck his finger in his mouth to clean off the remainder. Amy gaped at him "But isn't that...?"

"What, this? This is just guacamole. There's an ex-Californian hippie that makes it up for me special. I ran out of grease paint months ago." Since Amy didn't understand any of the nouns in that sentence, she just continued to gape, her small pearl-like teeth gleaming in the semi-darkness. "Here, I'll show you," and he dipped his finger one last time in the jar before moving it between her open lips. Instinctively she closed them around his finger, and her senses awoke to something marvelous. It was tangy, yet full, and she couldn't get enough of it.

"You know, I was always prepared to pay the ultimate sacrifice," he said with another grin, leaning in to lick a drop of guacamole that had settled into the corner of her mouth.

She swatted him in the arm. "Doesn't mean you still aren't going to die," she replied ominously but with a matching smile.

Somehow the jar slipped from his grasp and they fell into an embrace, oblivious to the cold stone of the floor or the approaching echo of muffled footsteps.

22

Showdown in the Lost City

They didn't have time to exchange more than a few kisses before the muffled footsteps resolved into an entire phalanx of black-clad bad guys visible through the grating at the other end of the subterranean passage. Plasma guns were in their hands and long knives hung from their belts. Priorities being what they were, the couple pulled back a few centimeters and tried to focus their attention on staying alive. Amy made an executive decision and took out the narrow silver whistle she'd been wearing around her neck. She put it to her lips and blew three silent blasts as she'd been instructed while Ten watched impassively. Then a thought struck her: "But if you've closed the nearby portals, how will they get here?" Dejected, she let the whistle fall back.

"The Leanadhe operate under their own set of rules. They have doors and portals that are built on magic, not technology, and they've had them far longer. It's just that the rest of us can't use them. You've done your best and asked for help; we'll just have to hope that they're in the mood to respond." He didn't sound very confident to Amy's ears.

Amy gathered herself together. "Right then, what now?"

"Let's see what your arm says." With that, he lifted her left arm and pushed back the sleeve gently.

Amy gaped and felt a little revolted that her own body was doing things she wasn't even aware of. For there on her arm, some of the tracings had re-formed into a compass. Tiny blue numbers were arranged around the outside. When she moved her arm in a different direction, the numbers shifted along the circle.

Ten smirked with satisfaction. "Thought so. I'd read about this but there weren't any pictures, so I wasn't sure how it would look."

"What is it?"

"Those numbers are the bad guys in each direction when you are the center." He did the math in his head. "Looks like 650, or thereabouts."

"Six hundred and fifty!"

"Or thereabouts, yes. What? You don't think we can handle that?" He looked downright happy.

Amy started to wonder if she knew him at all.

He traced the compass on her arm. "I should probably warn you that this isn't really about bad guys, just the ones that want to do you physical harm. It's not going to show you the bad guys that want to hurt other people, or even the good guys that might hurt you without meaning to." With that, he gave her one last kiss on the lips and pulled her back the way they had come. He stopped at a fork in the tunnel that Amy hadn't noticed before. He checked her arm again and smiled at the little green number (147) that was moving from the top to the side. "Guess those elves aren't so bad after all…"

With lightning speed, Ten pushed Amy behind him just as one of the mercenaries got out, "Hey! There's some-"

Ten's arm around his neck cut off anything further. Ten

pulled the body deeper into the shadows while Amy tried not to hyperventilate. Things had gotten a lot scarier with that. She hadn't expected company in the tunnel. Ten motioned for her to stay back while he waited for the first guy's friend. He didn't have to wait long.

"Ted? Ted, where you at?" a wandering flashlight beam was followed by mercenary number two, who wasn't quite as gung ho as number one but met a similar fate. Ten reached back for Amy's hand without turning his head. They hugged the walls in total darkness. "They're probably working in pairs, but no need to take chances."

"Won't they come looking for them?"

"Probably, but hopefully not for a while."

Back above ground, but somewhat trapped in the little building, Amy could see daybreak over the hills. She could barely make out the little black figures moving over the hills like ants. She shivered. How on earth could they survive this? Then she saw Master An under a tree just beyond the square. She touched Ten's arm and pointed, the question in her eyes. They both looked at the diminutive man, perfectly still under the tree. Then, with a force neither expected, Master An raised his staff high over his head horizontally and then pointed it at the far hill. Trees and dirt scattered across the landscape like shaking out a rug. Beneath all the detritus, a jade-green dragon unfurled itself and stretched. Its eyes popped open golden yellow and then a long forked tongue flicked out, and it ate fifty of the closest mercenaries. Being an Asian-style dragon, it didn't have wings, so picked its way delicately down the slope and settled itself in the patch of sunlight in the square.

The mercenaries scattered in whatever direction took them away from the giant beast. That is until it settled down to sun itself. Then, their radios squawking, several took up position and aimed their plasma guns. Amy clapped her hand over her mouth. But when the guns fired, the dragon did nothing more than stretch... and grow. Ten chuckled softly. "It's feeding on the energy." Apparently the mercenaries realized this too, because they stopped shooting and, based on the squawking over the radio, decided to regroup on the other side of the river. Suddenly the square and surrounding countryside was empty except for the dragon, now with half-lidded eyes. Amy checked her arm herself. The blue numbers had coalesced into one big number off to the left. The smaller green number was moving rapidly toward the center. With that, she looked up just in time to see the elven guard enter the square.

They gave the dragon a wide berth and then spread out into the shadows of the square, becoming nearly invisible as they did so. Gantnor walked directly to the door Amy was hiding behind and pushed it open. She fell back. He gave the crown an appreciative glance before bowing low. "Your excellence, we are at your service."

Not sure what the protocols were in this case, she merely inclined her head and said, "Thank you." As if his entrance had been a signal, everyone else materialized shortly thereafter and they all moved next door to the fire and food while the temporary calm prevailed. The dragon appeared to be asleep, but not the deep sleep that had previously caused him to grow trees.

There was a lot of quiet planning around the campfire that night. They decided they would get in position in the hour just before dawn and attack at first light. That would give them the optimal advantage to do as much damage as they could. Amy went to bed that night in the curve of Ten's arm and wished she could just revel in the moment. She drifted into an uneasy sleep and dreamed of giant rabbits and manifest destiny.

In the pre-dawn light, the archers took up their positions in the trees. They disappeared so completely that Amy had to squint to make out the faint blue glow of their beads. Master An was back in the square with the dragon going over the plan. Kalil, St. Abyn, and Ten took up a triangular position in front of Amy, who was, quite frankly, scared. She had known there would be danger in theory. But somehow she'd though it would be more like reading a gothic novel, where the scary parts don't interfere with confidence in the happy ending. She wasn't feeling like the happy ending was guaranteed just at the moment. She sighed heavily and tried to relax her shoulders.

Then all hell broke loose. Something must have given away their position, or perhaps the mercenaries had gadgets not unlike her arm compass, for an array of plasma fire started raining down on their heads. The dragon arrived and dealt with what he could, but much of the battleground was now in close combat and he couldn't get a clear shot. The crown gave Amy a warning tap on her left cheek. She turned to see a mercenary bearing down on her with a wicked knife. Without knowing why, she raised her left palm directly at him. He vanished in a puff of smoke. She looked down at her palm but couldn't see anything different. The crown gave another tap on her left cheek. She repeated the procedure. Pretty soon she was pointing and dispatching a fair number of the bad guys.

Her palm had a range of about twenty feet, so it was only good for those that got around her team's immediate perimeter. They too were speedily getting rid of mercenaries. Amy took a brief moment to check her arm and saw that the number had dropped to a mere fifty. When she looked up again, it was to see

Caroline in sleek black sneaking up on Ten from behind. She had a very large, non-technological rock in her hands, and it wasn't hard to figure out what she had planned. That was when Amy got mad. She walked up behind the blonde and put her palm directly on the back of her neck. Luckily, she and the rock disintegrated before she got a chance to drop it. Ten looked up just as it happened and left it at "thanks" before getting back to the business at hand. Except that somehow that seemed to have ended things. The last of the mercenaries were now hightailing it to a portal that had opened along the riverbank and were diving through it. In seconds, there was nothing left but the lingering smoke of plasma fire and bodies, most of them clad in black but a few in woodland brown.

23

The Empress Takes Her Throne

Amy took a deep breath and wiped the trail of muddy sweat off her forehead. Wisps of dust and steam from the plasma destabilizers were still drifting on the breeze above the ruins. The elven guard were manhandling the remaining mercenaries. Ten was checking Amy over for untreated wounds. He didn't find any but seemed reluctant to stop looking.

Lord Kalil had broken his leg in a daring leap from a second-story wall. He'd managed to flatten three bad guys at once, so it wasn't for nothing, but he was still muttering under his breath as his brother helped him hobble over to the others.

The little group watched as the elven guard, with their captives, disappeared through the portal. It had been agreed that they would be taken to a little, barely habitable planet that had only an elven door but no portal. They would live, but not enjoy it. Amy smiled with satisfaction at the thought. She had enough troubles without having to fend off constant assassination attempts.

A few hours later, everyone was relaxing back at their makeshift camp in the circle building on the square. Master An had seen to Kalil's leg and pressed a few compresses to everyone else's bruises. A formal elven escort had materialized to recover their fallen, but after a few ceremonial words with Amy they hadn't lingered. Ten had taken the two stuffed pink unicorns that the twins had won on the space station and positioned them on either side of the doorway as some sort of heraldic expression of victory. Master An had nodded his approval and said something about spirit guardians.

Amy sipped her cup of tea and wondered what came next. Would they just go their separate ways now? Could she just return home after everything that had happened? She didn't think she was the same person anymore.

The next morning, she found out. Emerging from the circle building still yawning and wincing at a few of the worst bruises on her hip, she stopped short at the overnight transformation of the square. A line of creatures—"people" definitely didn't cover it—snaked through the square and beyond. They were talking, squeaking, and waving tentacles amongst themselves as they waited. Amy blinked twice, but they were still there. First in line was a tall, slender, tree-like person who bowed low. "Empress Amy, I am Neerwin of the planet Aquanegus in the second time dimension. We rejoice in your re-opening of the Imperial City and wish to parlay a new treaty." At that, she (we think) bowed again and stepped aside. The next in line stepped forward on hoofed feet, placed a small covered bowl at Amy's feet, and said much the same thing. Amy gulped silently and thought frantically. She made her best effort to appear regal while realizing that this wasn't something she could delegate. During the two hours it took for the line to move past her and re-form on the other side of the square, the rest of our heroes had emerged, seen what was happening, and retreated again. Ten had pushed a cup of tea into her hand, but even he wasn't brave enough to face this much protocol.

When the last representative had moved aside, Amy made a lovely speech that she'd crafted while waiting, promising everyone that she was grateful for their coming and would they please set up individual appointments with her private secretary St. Abyn. She thought she heard a screech emanate from the building behind her at that, but with so many creatures present, who could be sure? She smiled and bowed to the crowd and went back inside.

"Now Amy, you can't do that—I have a business to run! I'm already way behind this quarter's projections."

Amy raised one eyebrow (she'd been practicing in front of a little mirror for weeks). "Yes, I can. You're the one that got me into this mess in the first place. If you hadn't interfered I'd be happily toiling away as a governess in some macabre castle."

St. Abyn didn't look convinced that the current situation was a downgrade from that dramatic picture, but after a whispered conversation with Kalil, he subsided and just muttered to himself every few minutes. Amy let him sulk. She knew he wouldn't be able to resist having his finger in that many interspecies pies. She sat down next to Ten and let her head fall onto his shoulder. His arm came up to hold her against his side. This was definitely better than being a governess.

Eventually they had that long-delayed talk. The one where Ten, now having realized that he wasn't going to have to die in battle after all, could finally tell Amy that he loved her. He expressed this with a higher proportion of kissing than words, and not quite as many allusions to her being an Incomparable as she had originally envisioned. She had to admit that, knowing him as she now did, she wouldn't have believed any flowery words from him anyway. That Ten immediately followed his declaration with the one hundredth reference to "making the ultimate sacrifice" had Amy glaring while simultaneously kissing him back enthusiastically.

They opted not to have a long engagement. An official envoy was quickly dispatched at Amy's behest to the Northern Wastelands to retrieve Wallace, the cat. When he arrived in his special chamois carry basket and Amy saw his torn ears and belligerent expression, she wasn't overly confident in her decision. But as soon as Wallace was released, he quickly sized up the situation and let Amy know that as fellow royalty she would be allowed to scratch his royal tummy. Amy was smitten.

Their wedding was the talk of the space-time continuum. Thanks to the reopened diplomatic channels (Amy's wrist was still tired from signing her full name so many times), it was covered on every network, mindspeak session, and other communications method simultaneously. Those who were republican at heart, and while happy to see balance restored to the cosmos wished it hadn't come with a return of a monarchy, took long vacations to the Northern Wastelands, which didn't get any communication regardless of the transmission type. Amy took her new responsibilities seriously, and so wanted to give the public what they were expecting. Hence, her wedding dress was literally fashioned of moonbeams accented with fairy lights (tiny fairies that had volunteered for the job, not the small bulbs with too much electrical cord often found masquerading under that name). Fatima did the dessert table. The rest was incidental and not much was remembered the following day, but everyone agreed they'd had a fabulous time.

For her going-away dress, Amy had chosen a soft pink silk with coquelicot ribbons drawn up under the bust with matching rosettes on the sleeves and hem. She'd had a bit of difficulty communicating her desires to the local dressmaker, who was used to making sleek, body-fitting cat suits with odd wingy bits here and there, depending on what was hot that season. Eventually she'd prevailed. She had not been able to find a bonnet, but since Ten had expressed and demonstrated a fondness for her freckles, she decided it wasn't necessary. It should go without saying that Ten wore khaki. To everything.

They honeymooned at Riparian Hall. It seemed that once Amy went missing and did not return compromised as Uncle Greg expected, her old nurse began asking awkward questions. And unless you should be lured into thinking old nurses have no influence, it should be known that this particular old nurse, before coming to the infant Amy, had been nurse to a boy who later became prime minister. That esteemed gentleman was also quite fond of Betsy and didn't like to see her worried. While nobody could actually prove it, the general consensus was that Uncle Greg had nothing of value to offer human society, so that prime minister arranged for him to be press-ganged from his gentleman's club in London. Even Uncle Greg thought it was a gag at the time and didn't put up much resistance until he was hogtied in the ship's hold. By then it was too late for him, but perfect timing for all his neighbors and acquaintances.

On a beautiful spring morning the day after their wedding, Ten and Amy arrived at the transport deep in the earth that had begun it all. He lifted her up to the first rung of the ladder and helped keep her long skirts from tripping her as she climbed. You rarely read of Regency misses climbing ladders because of this very problem.

Arriving at the hall, Amy was greeted by all her old staff, who kindly made allowances for Ten's poor fashion sense and appalling manners on the grounds that he had clearly made her happy, and so what else really mattered? Fires were laid in every room and Amy could feel the grasping spirit of Uncle Greg fade with every pop and crackle in the fireplace. Later that evening, in the very bedroom where Amy had planned her adventure, Ten did indeed show his willingness to make the ultimate sacrifice, several times. Rather annoyed with his teasing on the subject, Amy pointed out with asperity that according to the Latin, "ultimate" could only happen once. To which Ten replied, "I'm not dead yet, so I must not have it quite right," and prepared to try again. Amy had already decided that, despite the teasing, he'd definitely been worth waiting for, even though he was never as deferential as protocol demanded an Incomparable empress be treated.

Regency England was clearly not Ten's thing, but he endured it for Amy's sake and she, now also grown beyond its confines, asked only a brief visit every year to catch up with friends and the latest fashions. In turn, they spent a week every winter in the Northern Wastelands, avoiding the stew and visiting Master An, who had immigrated there to prove the power of good feng shui on the most recalcitrant of subjects.

Lord Kalil went on a quest of his own to find the pale green lady pastry chef. He periodically checked in with his friends and brother, but is still searching. St. Abyn settled into a permanent position as Amy's private secretary and chief of intelligence. He found stealing information to be not only easier, but more socially acceptable. It also required much less paperwork.

The End

Links

Did you enjoy this story? I would greatly appreciate your honest ranking and/or review on Amazon, Goodreads, or your favorite book review site.

Find out what's happening:
Website: http://books.JulietChase.com
Twitter: @julietchase
Facebook: www.facebook.co/JulietChasePage/

Or email me at: JulietChase.com@gmail.com I would love to hear what you liked (or not) and what you want to see next.

Also by Juliet Chase

Annabel's Dilemma (A short story introducing the Love@ Labresoft series)

The Love List (Book 1 of the Love@Labresoft series)

The Trouble With Mini Cows (Book 1 of the Fidalgo Island series)

www.ingramcontent.com/pod-product-compliance
Lightning Source LLC
Chambersburg PA
CBHW050848180626
46814CB00007B/2676

9 781939 361042